MYRA
STOLEN INNOCENCE

MYRA ZHIVANEVSKAYA

Ménage à Trois Publishing
www.menageatroispublishing.com

ISBN - 978-0-615-35991-5

To Ove...

The last of the true Vikings.

4 - MYRA

THE MAKING OF A SLAVE

I have heard it said by many that the slave chooses her owner, and that is her last choice. Perhaps, but in my experience I cannot say the same.............

Its almost been four years now since I first lay eyes on him, the man who ultimately was to rule my world and my very existence. He who would mold and shape me forever, for good or bad. It was at a family gathering on July four. That proud American day of national independence and patriotism. It was my family's and my extended family's custom to gather on this day. We did it every year. All were welcome, and there were often many who came to these occasions who had very little family association at all.

He was one of those guests, my father's friends son. A well traveled, aging, but vital Danish man who had currently been employed on a building project. He had thought to bring his youngest son with him that he might see more of the world and work as well. I was never formally introduced to him nor his father, my own father did not seem to think his wife or two daughters merited this pleasantry. That had always been his way. He was a man inhabiting a man's world and he never let us forget it.

It was a warm July day, the air thick with humidity, the brooding, building clouds on the far horizon a promise of evening deluge. My mother and I hoped it did not arrive sooner to spoil the day. I was fourteen that summer, my little sister was ten. My elder brother who was nineteen was nowhere in sight. I enjoyed catching up with my cousins, aunts, and uncles, most of us grateful for the fortune our new country had brought us. Yes, America the promised land, however the promise I feel had never really come to my parents as it had to other members of my family. My father had struggled here from the outset with his rigid inability to adopt new ways. As a result our fortunes had plummeted with him.

You must forgive me for I digress. The first image I have of him was nothing more than a smile, and what a smile it was, he was golden and handsome with piercing emerald eyes, like some fairy tale prince of my childhood stories. The woman was waking up in me, my body was changing and I had begun to really notice men in recent months in a very different way than I had ever viewed them before. However I was still in vast ignorance of the beast that lie beneath.

He asked me my name in his exotically accented voice, I had not expected him to. No one noticed Myra. I paused before I answered him, and he just smiled. "What a pretty name." He said. I noticed my mother glare at me most annoyed. I did not understand why I had displeased her. I was only trying to be polite, to appease her I made some feeble excuse I had to help with the food and left his presence.

The rain held off, I played with my sister and some of my cousins. I did not think of him any further. As the day wore on I sought the shade of the trees in the reserve, it was hot and oppressive and I sat with a cool drink savoring it and deeply dwelling on my lot. I had of recent months not been content to 'go play' as my parents put it. I wanted to be part of the adult world, and do adult things. I was on the precipice of being torn between the two worlds in my crossover into adult hood. I found I would now often seek solitude to contemplate things, and I would walk alone.

On this day I did just that, I knew this area well. The stretches of swamp land that lie between the white sandy beaches and the seeping back waters were my home. I was so engrossed in my little world I had not noticed him. He had been swimming, he was clad only in pair of shorts, a colorful beach towel carelessly draped over his rippling shoulder. His great blonde mane was wet with the sea, which today resembled the color of his eyes. He smiled and approached me, he was pleasing to look at and intimidating all in the same glance. "I never got the chance to tell you my name." He said as he sauntered closer, an easy smile on his face. I smiled back, I could see he was alone. I felt shy and small, but curious also. He walked right up to me looked me in the eyes, I wanted to look away but I found I could not. He was a very arresting man.

Perhaps if I had reacted differently I could have undone the course of my destiny, but little did I know that then. "My name Myra, is Master." I did not understand. I was sure I had misheard him, but with his heavy accent I was most unsure. He looked over my shoulder, I turned to see what he was looking at, but there was no one there. He put his arms about me and my eyes opened wide. "Shhhh Myra." He said. I should have shouted but I did not, I do not know why I did not. He escorted me off the pathway into the bushes. I could not work out what he wanted. My mother had told me many times not to go running off alone with boys or I would be sorry, but he was no boy he was a grown man. I could not understand what he wanted with me?

I remember vividly his hand hard on my arm, he touched the side of my face ever so softly it tickled. No one noticed Myra, why had he? I did not understand, and the way he was intensely looking at me unnerved me completely. "I have to go now." I stammered, I did not like this game. It felt wrong, very wrong. "Mom will be looking for me."

"Not yet." Was all he said. To my horror he reached his warm hand under my dress. I could smell the sea salt in his hair. He reached in to my panties and pushed his large finger into a place I until then had never fully realized I had. It hurt and I made little whimpering noises as I twisted on his invading finger my face burrowed into his chest. "Good girl." He persuaded. "Be still and listen." It was hard to, his assault on my insides was all I could think of. "You little Myra are marked for me, I have watched you from the first. One day you will be my little slave girl, that I promise." His voice was quiet almost a whisper as he pressed his huge warm body against mine. "Now if I let you go you are not to tell a soul, not your sister, not your mother, no one. If you do I will find you, and I will hurt you. It's our little secret understood?" I nodded, agreeing to anything to be gone from him and this place.

Freed from his grasp I ran from the woods back to the safety of the gathering. No one had even noticed my absence. I guessed this is what my mother had meant about boys, and suddenly I could see the wisdom in her words. Though in my naivety I could still not really fathom what it was he had done to me, nor why.

I did not see him again for almost two weeks, But the July four interlude had left an indelible impression on my mind. I did not tell anyone, but kept 'our' little secret. Part of me, the girl who never got noticed was indeed flattered by his attention. I had never been noticed by anyone I liked in my life, except perhaps by a succession of unappealing, pimply faced boys from high school; but this exotic, golden man, he had noticed me. I had begun to daydream of him and he became in an oblique fashion my handsome prince that would rescue me from my disjointed unhappy family, and my woes.

He surprised me as I rounded the corner on the busy street packed with summer tourists. I felt startled and a little nervous but as we were in a public place I knew I was quite safe. He had dirty work clothes on and was covered in concrete dust, even through this he still shone. "Hello Myra." Again the arresting smile. I smiled up at him and paused. It was all he needed. "I have something for you he said." As he fumbled in his blue jeans pocket. There were people pressing past us oblivious to our little interlude. He placed a tiny maroon box in my hand with gold metal edges. I gasped. "Open it he encouraged." I did slowly, to reveal a delicate little silver ring with an enameled bluebird on it. I had never received a gift like this. This was to me a girl of fourteen a serious adult gift. "It's the bluebird of happiness, for you. The most beautiful girl in the world." He said. I did not know what to say.

I hid the little box containing the ring down the bottom of my jewelry box, buried deep beneath the cheap brightly colored baubles of my fleeting childhood. I longed to wear it but I did not dare, fearing it would raise too many unanswerable questions. Instead just peeking at it furtively when my sister was nowhere about. I felt like a jewel thief who had in my possession a stolen diamond.

The next time I encountered him was a few days later, again in a public setting. He called to me as I was crossing a car park near his work site, I must confess I had not happened this way by accident. I had hoped to at least catch a glimpse of him. This time he beckoned me to his work truck. I was wary, and he presented me with a beautiful silver bracelet, on the inside of it was etched the words 'My slave.' He placed the bracelet on my wrist, I had numerous others and it blended in with them. I had decided that I would already wear it, and not hide it away as I had shamefully done with his previous gift.

"I see you do not wear my ring?" He commented looking at my fingers adorned with numerous cheap ones. I was embarrassed he had noticed and did not know what to say. "You did not like it?" He questioned.

"Oh, no, no, not at all, I loved it." I replied feeling ever so awkward.

"But you prefer these to mine?" Again he gestured at my hands. I felt I had slighted him, and worse still belittled his beautiful gift. I mumbled something equally foolish about not wanting to risk losing it. All he said was, "Myra we cannot go through life fearful of what me might lose."

In August I saw him many times, always in public. He did not do anything untoward or the least bit improper as he had done in the reserve that day, and the summer came to a close. I learned his name was Frej Eriksen, and I believe he was twenty-four. Ten years my senior. I saw him often, he gave me many gifts, sometimes candy, but most of all he made me feel special and beautiful. Hence our dangerous and forbidden liaison blossomed..........

The Alabama summer heat, the beach, white clean sands, blue skies, the colorful planked beach houses, and the hubbub of the endless stream of tourists that pass me by. I see him, he looks at me as I pass, capturing me in the thrall of his vibrant stare, he smiles lazily and shows his perfect white teeth. He is unshaven, sporting the stubble of many days, and he is warm, it is too warm for him here; patches of perspiration beneath the arms of his light blue work shirt attest to his discomfort. He is taking a beer at an outside table of the Shrimp Basket. He does not come there for the seafood, but only to watch passers by and drink. It is indeed a perfect location for such sport, and I know he has been waiting for me.

I pause, I always do, I don't want anyone I know to see me with him. Its not that I would be ashamed, its more I know what I engage in is forbidden. Rumors travel fast in this small tourist town, my parents do not need to know. Yes, I am beginning to grow up, and I'm also beginning to accumulate secrets. A small feeling of excitability in my stomach, as I walk beneath the shade of the veranda and sit down at his table. I decide to maintain some distance, yet part of me yearns to sit close and touch him. It would not be seemly at only fourteen, with him being a grown man, and even though we are surrounded by tourists with not a familiar local face in view I do not wish to be noticed. This is a dangerous liaison, but I find I am inextricably drawn.

So as a consolation I sit opposite him, he smiles at me wolfishly, his rugged charm most irresistible. He leans forward, I feel so small before him, his hands fascinate me. So large and strong, and I think of them on me and inside me as he did that day at the party in the nature reserve, not so far from these white shores.

His arresting emerald eyes alight on a young waitress as she passes by our table, she stops and asks him what he wants. He captivates all in his path. It is so enticing to at last be drawn into the world of adult intimacies. My skin tingles, and so do other forbidden places as I sit attempting to appear indifferent to my companion opposite. The waitress brings a menu and sets it before me, she smiles. She is not that much older than I, he is looking at her as a lion views his pride. Yet at that moment I was so young, so untried in the bounds of love, and the wiles of a man, especially an insatiable, deviate man like Frej Eriksen to truly see.

This time I will not disappoint him, I proudly display his gifts. I have chosen clothing that he might like, my tightest pair of jeans and my black top with the plunging neckline. I so desire to please him above all things. I'm hungry, I don't get much opportunity to eat out, and there had been nothing at home to eat but stale Cheerios for breakfast. Unappealing indeed. Last night only heated up leftovers and the acrimony of my parent's arguments to fill me. I order, hesitantly, though I am hungry I am also so nervous its difficult to eat. I sense he is being very careful in public. I want to touch him beneath the table, to feel the large solidarity of his muscled frame. He downs the mug of pale beer which he affectionately dubs 'water' an a few easy gulps and orders another, he is not looking at my face but at my cleavage, my cheeks burn under his observation.

His eyes say one thing, his words say another. He sits, burning me with his animal gaze, uttering small talk. I do the same twisting my hands in my lap, I am looking at the ring he has so recently gifted me. The one I hide from my parents and my sister, as a tainted thing. My heart pounds he is everything I have always fantasized about, part actor, part rock star, part fairy tale prince. Yet he is a normal man, a man who works his days building with steel and mortar. I know I cannot stop this game he has enacted.

The sea air, the light cooling breeze washes over us. Seagulls fly close looking for opportune meals, noisy in their quest. I had been afraid, and confused after the interlude in the reserve. So soon those feelings have transformed into blind infatuation. At times in fleeting moments of clarity I would question my actions and my feelings, only to push them aside in favor of the idea this was nature and as all earthly things he and I were bound to its calling. I wanted more, yet I was unsure what more entailed. He knew, he could be my teacher and I his willing disciple. I wanted him to show me what a few of my friends told me they knew; though I suspected they really did not. Yes, I was ready. I burned to know the things my mother had only hinted at.

My sandaled foot collided with his leg under the table, my painted toes lingered daringly beneath the frayed hem of his jeans touching his shin with flirtatious desire. His eyes locked on mine, the smallest hint of a one sided smile graced his rugged face. A smile in time I would come to intimately know. I wondered what he was thinking? Oh such dangerous adoration.

In those closing days of summer hurricane Katrina struck, needless to state it is common knowledge the destruction was widespread and very costly. Fearful of the intensity of the storm my family did not stay, we went to my Aunt's home in Columbus Ohio. To us three siblings it was an exciting change of pace from the sleepy tourist town of Gulf Shores, my first time in a real big city. Everything to me seemed fast and furious, and I kept thinking the sea would be just around every corner. My parents did not share our enthusiasm, they seemed glued to the radio or the television trying to ascertain what was happening at home.

When we did return to the site of our family home it was a sobering vision, our domicile bore little resemblance to the one we had left. My parents never had much to begin with, and this I believe caused their already often resignedly bitter relationship to further deteriorate. Most of our home's contents were water damaged or blown away, as the roof had been torn from it in the hurricane. I could sense my mother's thorough sense of desolation as she quietly picked through the remnants of her life, searching for anything that might be salvaged. It was a very difficult time.

Mr. Eriksen and his handsome son had not chosen to evacuate during the hurricane, they leased a place further inland that had been for the most part unscathed. Kindly he offered us a place to stay until our home could be rebuilt, my father accepted grateful for some breathing room. I felt excited in the pit of my stomach, yet a little fearful to. I could not believe this ill fortune had placed me in such close proximity to the man I now vividly fantasized about. Most of my friends dreamed of rock stars or actors, but I had the real thing, and he was now living on my doorstep.

The Eriksen's compound for that's what it was, consisted of twenty acres of mostly treed land and undulating red sand. There was a long driveway leading in to the property, the buildings were not visible from the road. It looked like a place to me that two lone men might live. There was no attempt at a garden or even a neat lawn, just a robust collection of weeds that were occasionally cut to stem their unruly, rampant growth. Scattered around the two homes were many discarded trucks, cars, and old appliances. We all had to be careful where we played lest one cut themselves on some hidden piece of steel buried in the long grass. There were two singlewides that faced one another in an angular fashion that formed a loose V. Mr. Eriksen was only too happy to let us live in one, saying we could stay for as long as we wished.

My parents had always fought, but here the altercations became even more violent and heated. Through the thin walls late at night, my sister sleeping soundly close by I could hear father hitting her and mother crying bitterly. I loved my parents, but I had never felt truly close to either of them. My mother lived most of her life going from one Doctor's appointment to the next. Blindly seeking validation, or at the very least acceptance of the life she could not change. Tranquilizers had long been her friend. My father did not seem to care, perhaps in his mind he was satisfied her addiction made her more malleable and more dependent on him. I never saw him act cruelly toward her in the open, his many threats were implied, and mostly missed by children's ears. However behind closed doors father had no compunction enforcing his law by violence, to the rest of the world he hid it well. He was an unapproachable, taciturn man. He believed all females were his inferiors and designed for a background role only. He doted on my eldest brother Dmitry, his only son, he was unashamedly his pride and joy. I always wondered why he did not stop having children after his first one? As he had no interest in us two girls, period.

During our stay at the Eriksen's while my parent's wrestled with the recalcitrant insurance company, and bickered incessantly between themselves, I saw the handsome Frej Eriksen often. Disturbingly I soon realized he had distanced himself from me. I felt hurt and abandoned, it was as though he did not see me any more. I found I was now chasing him for his attention, finding reasons to single him out. Both he and his father worked for long periods also, almost seven days a week. There was an avalanche of building work right now after the hurricane, and I am sure the two men made a very lucrative income.

As fall ripened into it's balmy fullness and my fifteenth birthday rapidly approached it happened, the event that was I believe the making of my slavery. The day was a beautiful one, it was just after lunch on a Sunday. My father and brother were out working, doing clean up, there was a lot of extra money to be made at this. My mother had a planned get together with her girlfriends and she left my sister and I, as she often did, at home alone. We were watching television, nothing out of the ordinary just some cartoons. I felt restless and bored and wished we lived closer to town as I missed walking there and meeting with my friends. I did not feel at all like being my sister's baby sitter.

Mr. Eriksen had left at first light that morning, but this day his son had not accompanied him. I could see Frej sitting alone on the deck drinking, he had been there all day stretched out in the sun. I often would stand at the glass door and daydream out the window, I longed to be anywhere but here. I think at fourteen most of us share this pass time daydreaming about the big unknown future ahead, filling it with all kinds of imaginary things. My heart fluttered as I saw him cross the yard, there was no mistaking he was coming here. He knocked on the door, his knuckles heavy on the sliding glass. I tried to act as though I was in no hurry, and to appear that I was not at all overeager to see him, but the actress in me was still only a little girl, with none of nuances of the woman I would yet become.

He smiled as I opened the door, a self assured smile that said I can see through you little Myra. He looked to me like a magnificent lion, the afternoon sun on his golden hair and his tanned skin. I let him inside, my sister was captivated by the cartoons and she barely paid him any heed. However I could not say the same, he had my full attention. I no longer felt afraid of him as I had that confused day at the reserve when he had caught me in the trees. Since then he had been nothing but kind to me, and the fear I had felt for him had long ago dissipated. I saw him gaze over at my sister, she was engrossed, and I saw him look long out of the doorway towards his father's abode and down the driveway. He asked me where my parents and brother were and I told him without any hesitation. "They won't be back till late." I said, "but I have to stay here and look after my sister." In my innocence I had no thought of what this predator had in store.

He stood there in the living room for some time. He seemed to be weighing some important decision in his mind. I felt a small tendril of fear as he stood there quietly, his emerald eyes looking at me but not at my face. I offered to get him a drink but he declined. He put his hand on my arm as he did that hot July day at the reserve. His grip had a sense of urgency, beer on his breath. I stiffened, he looked me in the eye, but he said nothing, nor did I. My mistake perhaps? I often wonder what he might have done if I had of made a fuss? I realize now looking back at that moment he was waiting to see if I reacted negatively to his initial advance. However in my passive ignorance I only gave him the cue he was seeking.

I have always been a very submissive and shy person, the kind who makes for easy prey. I know that now, but I did not know myself then. He took one more glance at my sister, she had her dolls on the floor and was lost in the cartoon. He obviously decided in that moment he would make his move. He directed me to our shared bedroom, it felt most strange to be standing in this familiar place with him blocking the door. Even my father and brother never ventured here, this was a girls only place. I did not know what he wanted of me, and whatever it was I did not want my little sister to be privy to it, or involved. I resigned myself as he came close and began touching me to let him do what he wanted. I would be good and quiet and my sister would never know, he would leave and everything would be all right.

He was silent as he caressed me on my budding breasts, pinching the nipples. I was confused and frightened as he toyed with my body generating feelings I had never before felt, and could not understand. He undid the zipper on his jeans and I was both awed and afraid to see how large he was. I had seen small boys naked many a time, but never a fully grown man, let alone an erect and lustful one. I had little time to fathom the mechanics of this. He pushed his fingers inside of me as he had the time before. He was less hesitant this time and rougher. I did not fight him though I still squirmed making every attempt at silence. I could discern the movie playing in the other room. On such a beautiful day the bedroom window was open and I could hear the birds singing in the trees beyond, and the ever present cicadas. The background music to summer here.

I watched his desire transform him, he had gone from meditational silence to rapid breathing, from gentle and confident, to forceful and rabid. He guided me backwards on to my sister's bed with great urgency, it was the closest to him. I did not feel comfortable with this as it was not my bed. He pressed me down on my back pulling my panties off and threw them on the floor. The bed was small with him on it, he was hot and heavy on top of me. Fear sparked in me then. I realized I should never have let him push me on to the bed. I made to reverse my decision, something primal told me he was going to hurt me.

I was no match for his strength or experience. He held me pinned beneath him with ease. He was fumbling with his crotch, that was when I first felt his hardness pressing into me. This was too much. I panicked and I made to scream. His large hand was on my mouth in an instant, his stubbled cheek pressing against my own. His long, thick, golden hair shielding my vision as it tumbled over my face.

"Shhhhh Myra." He rasped. "Be a good girl, you don't want me to hurt your sister do you?" I really do not know if he had meant this or not, but I did not want to find out. I felt him push harder, it was a tight pressing pain. I found try as I might I could not lie still, I fought it and struggled. He did not relent, his hand firm on my mouth, my legs spread wide, his own body like iron pressing between them. The more I fought the more he pressed into me. I felt he would tear me asunder, my eyes tearful with the hurt. For a brief moment he stopped and lay on me quite still, the pain inside me was there, but bearable. I thought, oh good it's over, but he was not finished. He began to rhythmically move back and forward in me. Again I panicked, it hurt immensely and my legs began to shake uncontrollably. "It's all right Myra it always hurts the first time, you are new." He quietly informed me. He never took his hand from my mouth, he did not trust me to be silent.

Just as I thought I could take his hurt no more, he suddenly pulled out of me, his hand left my mouth, and to my shock and disgust he came all over my exposed stomach. It was sticky and whitish and smelled disgusting. I lay there looking up at him like a wounded animal. He stood at the end of the bed pushing his semi flaccidness back into his jeans, and arranging his clothing. He wiped his semen from me with some of my clothes, lingering on my flat stomach in a gesture of silent admiration. I was crying silent tears, I did not understand. He pulled my dress down tenderly to cover my nakedness and looked at me and smiled. "Your a very good girl Myra." Something my father never said. He patted me on the cheek.

I sat up and looked down at myself, in recent weeks since our first interlude at the reserve I was very curious about the female part of me. It was yet new and undiscovered, it had only been a few months since I had had my first period, and I really until this day had a very fuzzy idea of what sex entailed. Now I knew. I realized with a start I was bleeding, he saw the look on my face as I examined the fresh blood on my fingers. "It's quite all right." He assured. "It proves to me you are new." He smiled his expansive smile as he crouched down by the bed kissing me on the forehead most tenderly. "Next time it wont hurt as bad, and eventually it will feel very, very, good. I promise Myra." I nodded in silence my lips were dry, my eyes sore from crying. "Now I must go, but remember Myra this is our little secret." Again I nodded, and as I had promised I never told a soul.

I began to retreat from my friends, not pay attention to my studies at school. Not that I was ever the most devoted student. I forged my parent's signatures on to the teacher's notes that were beginning to find their way home in profusion. Often I did not even brother to attend school at all. My family were busy with their own troubles and did not notice the changes in me or my behavior, least of all chide me over them. He was more blatant now and more insistent, he made me call him Master and not use his given name. I knew only very bad girls did what I was doing. Yes, I knew the kind, the ones who left school suddenly, took drugs, and had babies as teenagers, and I was so afraid he would tell my entire family especially my father. I could not live with that shame.

On the home front things were worsening as well. My parents were bordering on a divorce, my eldest brother moved out he could not take the living conditions. My sister and I suffered through this time, as my parents ran off the rails. Progress was slow on the rebuilding of our home, and it was harrowing to them.

He was right, yes it hurt at first, but in time the hurt gave way to feelings of euphoria and insatiable lust. I found I wanted him, needed him, it was as if he had broken a dam wall, and I was powerless to stem the tide. He noticed me, loved me, and craved my presence, and Myra the girl who was never noticed ate it all up and begged for more.

Just a few days after my fifteenth birthday which to me had been a disappointing non event, Master was using me in the cabin of his truck. It was late in the afternoon we were stretched out across the bench seat, he was hot on top of me, oblivious in his quest for desire. I was sticking uncomfortably to the vinyl upholstery enjoying the man he was in all his magnificence, when to my abject horror I saw my mother looking at me as I glimpsed her over his broad shoulder. I had no idea she had returned home. He never noticed in his lust, and I did not tell him. She just gave me a cold glare and walked away. Her look of resigned disapproval burned me, and I can still see her to this day. I guess she had hoped she had raised her daughter better. I felt I had selfishly failed her.

She never broached the subject of that dreadful day, at least not directly. I found I could no longer look her in the eye. She came to my room the next morning with a little box of birth control pills. She calmly sat with me on my bed and explained how and why it was so very important I use them and not forget to take a single one. That I felt was the day I entered womanhood.

My parents moved back into their new home taking my sister early that winter. My father did not care that I stayed behind. I think he was only to glad to not have the worry of supporting me, and my mother who knew my dreadful secret made no move to inspire me to leave. I guess in her mind she had decided it was my choice to make. Mr. Eriksen had left for Denmark just before citing family reasons, but his son stayed, there was plenty of work and he was living a good life.

Once Mr. Eriksen and my family departed it was quiet for a time, just he and I. Any pretense at school attendance was quite forgotten and I found I spent most of the days in his absence wandering the sea shore on the gulf, or staying home and keeping house. It was then he began to teach me his ways in seriousness, insisting I kneel naked before him when he returned from work. To begin with I did not take this as a serious command, but learned very swiftly through the application of his belt it was indeed an unbending request. That was the first time he ever beat me. He simply tied me over his bed and let me have the strap. There was no one about, no one to hear my wails of pain and pitiful begging for him to stop. I am sure to him they were just love taps, but to me they were ten of his best. I was sore on my behind for many days even the bones ached. I resolved right then I must listen up and adhere to his fancies far better than I had been.

During this time also he began to invite many of his friends to his home. Most of them young as he was. American boys and men who were rough and ready and worked on the building sites with him. I met them all, served them drinks, lit their cigarettes, and made them coffee to help with their hangovers, and attempted to play the part of the perfect hostess. Master fed me, clothed me, and filled my time and my body with his never ending desire.

My mother would visit regularly mostly while he was at work, she was quiet and tactful. She, as I, never very artful at confrontation, and much remained unspoken between us. I guess she visited just to observe I was well looked after and happy with my less than socially acceptable living arrangement. If people spoke ill of me, and I am sure they did she never let on. I knew she had deep issues herself, sometimes she would get out of her car and I would see the black eye, or the fact she had been crying endless tears. However as the months wore on she could see no evidence I was being mistreated and she seemed satisfied, even happy for me. My father never visited, he seemed to have no further interest in me at all. The only time I saw him was if he was in the car with my mother, and he was as always in a hurry to be gone.

Winter passed and so did spring. Master would often take me with him in his battered work truck. I was so happy by his side it could have been a limousine. It was of course limited the places we could go with me being underage, but I did not fail to notice how other women would look at him. Older women, but he was all mine. For the first time I felt I had something no one else did, that shining cut above.

Summer blossomed, the gulf ready and edgy as hurricane season approached, but it was to be a quiet summer. I cannot say the same. The visits of his friends had become increasingly rowdy, and frequent. During this time I learned that Master had a penchant for heavy drinking. Not just light beer either. I have never seen a man consume the volumes of strong alcohol I had seen him stow away. He could out drink any of the American men with no effort, he seemed to enjoy drinking them all under the table. To begin with this was amusing to watch, but I noted with some fear that even though he protected me from his drunken friends he was becoming less diligent in this, even delighting in it.

After one particularly bad weekend late that June I no longer felt I would be safe, I confronted him over it. I told him I would leave, I did not know how as I did not have a car but I intended to just the same. Until this time I guess I had only seen tiny snippets of the beast within. He looked sideways at me through his wild blonde mane, his one green eye firmly fixed on me. I saw him snarl baring his teeth, he had pointed canines like a wolf. He turned, his hands alighting on my throat wrapping them about my neck. I was not expecting this. I froze under his threatening grasp. He pressed my throat, not hard, but enough to begin to reduce my air intake. I stood very still, I did not wish to further incite him.

"Don't you listen to what I tell you girl?" He snarled menacingly. I could not help thinking he looked like a wild animal. "YOU ARE MINE!" He exploded angrily, shaking me. I clawed at him but he did not notice, his eyes bored into mine and I desisted. He never took his hands from my throat. "Do I really need to show you, just how much you are mine?" He growled. Silence was my friend. I had learned during his sudden, savage, anger attacks to remain passive. If I did not fight him he would calm down and he would stop.

"So Myra why am I with you? I ask myself that. I could have any woman I wanted." He teased, though I had to agree he probably could. His rough hands left my throat, his index finger stuck into my breastbone, hard. "Look at you, red neck trailer trash girl. I know what they call you. Too skinny, cries too much, no tittes. No idea how to really please a man...... Yes, Myra, why am I with you?" I did not know what to say I looked down at his bare feet, and I had to say I was suddenly fearful he would abandon me. I felt his large hand under my chin he was lifting my face to look into his. He was so much taller than I. I had to look right up. "Be a good girl Myra or I will get a better one, that I promise."

I did something I have not done since. I broke from his hand and ran out into the trees. Anywhere to be away from him. I heard him run part way after me yelling for me to return. I screamed and wailed, and cut myself on the brush and branches. When my tirade abated I lay in the warm sand exhausted and crying a flood of bitter tears. I was determined he would not just use me and throw me away.

July four, and this year at our annual party I was not the Myra of the year before. I no longer played with my cousins. I felt all grown up. However things with my family were very estranged, and Master and I did not stay for more than a polite visit. Besides he had other plans for the day.

The road to the river shack wound back into the swampy bayou, the trees hanging with Spanish moss, dense and dark. Master said he often came here to fish, he caught good catfish here, something I had never liked to eat myself. I was not crazy about fishing be honest, but he liked it so I aquiesed deciding to bring a good book to pass the time. Three of his work friends were already there, their lines in the water, drinking beer. It was not long before the other two of his friends arrived and they all sat on the muddy bank talking, backs to me, smoking, drinking, and catching very few fish. I must admit I felt like a spare prick at a wedding and wished I had of stayed home.

Master would every now and then turn to look at me as I sat on my chair reading my book, bothered by the plethora of insects. I really did not like fishing, but since that day we had argued, if you could even call it that. I really felt pressure to please him. I sincerely hoped he had noticed.

He had been there about an hour and I could sense he was impatient, and I hoped he might be considering going home. He rose from his chair and smiled at me, he had the capacity to make me melt every time. He led me into the dilapidated river shack, if it was indeed anyone's it had not been frequented for a very long time. It was small, just a single room and mostly made of iron, little more than an old tool shed on pylons. Even in the shade it was decisively warm within. The floor was made of well worn wooden planks and in it's centre stood an old iron double bed, sporting a very threadbare and soiled innerspring mattress. He looked at me and at the bed. There was no way I wanted to lay there, it was filthy and I am sure it was crawling with bugs. "Not here." Was all I said softly hoping he would listen, he was not very good at it.

"Wait here." Was all he said. I figured he was at the very least going to the truck to get a blanket.

He returned not with the hoped for item but some lengths of rope. I began to shake my head and repeat to him my request. "No not here." This place was filthy and nasty and I was not going to do this. He made me. I initially tried to be quiet about it. I did not wish to be viewed by any of his friends. He made me remove all my clothes then bound me to the bed with brutal efficiency. As I lay there I wondered why I let him do this, what was it deep inside that I got out of his treatment? However I knew what it was, he fueled my own self loathing, he validated the hate I already had for myself.

Satisfied he had me tied well he sat by me. I could not take my eyes from the door. I was so panicked one of his friends would walk in at any moment, but they did not. "Remember what we talked about the other day?" He prompted. How could I forget? I nodded. I wanted to keep this as quiet as possible. My skin was already crawling and itching from contact with the repulsive mattress. I was paying more attention to it than I was to him. "It's time to test your devotion to me, my little slave trash girl." These words so calmly spoken seized my interest. I feared where this might lead. "Now my request is simple." He stated it plainly like he was merely asking me to do no more bring him a coffee. "I want you to pleasure my five friends out there."

"Noooo" was all I could say. He slapped my face as I said it. It was a forceful stinging slap, they had to have heard it outside.

"That my slave is a word I, NEVER want to hear from your mouth. UNDERSTOOD!" He pressed his fingers hard into the sides of my face and shook my head, his jagged, dirty nails bit into the soft skin on my cheeks leaving marks. I nodded in affirmative, anything to placate him, my mind furiously working to extract myself from this and swiftly. "A slave has no choice. She just does!" He got up and walked from the door.

I will never forget that terrible afternoon, nor the lasting ramifications of the choice I made to evade his order. I made it out of inexperience and fear, and in hindsight it was the wrong choice, and has cost me dearly. He sat imperiously in the old chair in the far corner, he ordered me to pleasure them all with my mouth. I was still quite new to this and to be honest I found it a little icky even with him. Maybe that was why he tried to make me do it. I will never know, and I will never ask.

I had already decided I would not, and he could not make me. It was one thing doing such intimate things with him, my beloved, but they were not for anyone else. So when his first friend attempted to make such use of my mouth I summarily bit him. He could not get away from me fast enough, calling me every vile insult under the sun as he did so, holding his wounded organ. I really never intended to hurt him, at least not damage, I only wanted to just warn him enough to make them stop. Master's look was one of dire danger, and it was then I realized I was messing with something well beyond my feeble control.

His friends stood back by the wall, they were now very reluctant to continue the game, their impetus quite gone. Master rose from his place and calmly crossed the floor. The old boards creaked under his weight. Even in the confining ropes I shrunk away from him, I could feel his black vitriol as I had never felt it before. "I'll teach you Myra, to learn to unquestioningly do as I say." He said quietly. His friends were soberingly silent, all eyes engaged on the two of us. Thinking back on it I am not sure any of them were ready for what indeed transpired.

The blade was long thin, and very sharp. It was a fishing knife, he produced it from his boot and waved it before my eyes. Some of his friends had already regained their voice and were not slow in offering suggestions as to what he should do with it. It appeared though he was only focussing on me, he never answered them or looked at them. His breathing was slow and heavy, his wild, angry eyes on me making me feel so very small.

"You slave, refuse to give the gift of pleasure you were made for to my friends." He touched the cold steel to my chest between my breasts, the tip poked into my breastbone. For one wild instant I thought my life was over. I would be found dead here in this sorry place. Branded in death with the stigma of being the unfortunate foolish girl, the town slut who was murdered and no one cared about. However he slid the blade slowly across my flesh, almost erotically downward to my belly. He gazed back at me from the knife, he looked almost sorry. "What value is your gift Myra if you do not share it with others?" His voice was low, and tinged with sadness.

All I uttered was a small incoherent sound as the knife pricked me on the belly. He leant over me and I felt his fingers in me, I could not see what he was doing. His friends were making lewd suggestions and I was sure it was only a matter of time before he let them fuck me, one by one.

"I'm going to teach you Myra that when I say, you will be open to others of my choosing." I saw some of the men looked away, though a couple of them seemed to be most interested in whatever Master was doing to me. I felt something cold and hard pass into me. I figured it was the handle of the blade. I could cope with that, he had done things to me like this on many occasions, humiliating; but I assured myself it would be quite safe. It was then it occurred to me what he had really done. He had inserted the entire length of the sharp blade in me. I wanted to panic and struggle but was all too aware if I clamped down the razor sharp knife would only damage me all the more. I could feel it cutting me already, at least I thought so, it was hard to tell. He pressed across my belly holding me still, not that I needed any encouragement to do so. I froze hardly daring to even breathe. In a barely audible voice I begged him to take it out. I begged him not to hurt me. I told him I would be good and do as he said. All he need do was give me just one more chance. The dull pain inside was beginning to become sharper, more insistent. I felt very wet.

Two of his friends actually left the river shack, the other three watched uncertainly they too finally leaving us alone. He withdrew the knife, I felt it cut me as he pulled it out and it was now unmistakable, the wetness I could feel was blood, my blood. It was on me, the knife, and him. I began to scream.

The rest of the events of that day for me were somewhat blurred. I completely lost it in the river shack. I remember him slapping at me and trying to shut me up. The awful drive in the truck and me bleeding all over the bench seat and the blanket. The emergency room and it's rushed chaos, harsh lights, and confusion. An elderly white haired Doctor sitting between my legs and stitching me all up, telling me I was very lucky as I had been almost cut completely through. To his credit Master did not drop me and leave, but then he had recently assumed his legal status as my guardian. It would not have been seemly. Even through my haze I could see him looking at me hoping I did not betray him with what he had done.

I could have, and it all would have ended right there and then. However I found I could not do so. I had a heady cocktail of fear and love for this unpredictable man. I am sure I am not the first woman in the world to do this, nor the last. I simply told the Doctors, nurses and even the police officer that came to see me I had been investigating some kinky play with a boyfriend, and it was as much my fault as his. They wanted to know who this young man was, Master even pretended as my guardian he wanted to as well.

My recovery was difficult and slow, on leaving the hospital I found Master had to lift me into his truck as I could not step up. Walking was painful, I could not squat down, going to the toilet even worse. I was afraid every time I did I might tear myself open. They gave me painkillers but I am proud to say I never used them. Of course sex was out of the question also, but Master was not happy with this and did not let me rest for the prescribed time. He was already using me two weeks later. The first time I was fearful, he was careful but I did not wish him to. It hurt immensely and it bled badly. This did not daunt him though he felt sex was his entitlement, and after that day at the shack I was not going to tell him otherwise. The worse thing though was not the pain as I had expected it to be. It was his admission I no longer felt as good to him as I used to. I wept bitter tears at his words.

My sixteenth birthday came and went, Master pierced my navel. We both liked the way it looked. Things again settled down between us, but sadly for me the joy of sex was forever ruined. My injuries healed but not cleanly, often causing me great discomfort during our love making. I found I now spent most of it in damage control trying to get past the mounting pain to please him. I can no longer orgasm through penetration either. In recent years my difficulty has lessened a little but for the most part the pain is always somewhat present.

That November Mr. Eriksen's lease ran out on the place I had called home for just over a year. Master decided he would take the offer of a friend of his, to move into his beach house and cohabit with him. The place it's self was beautiful, a large sprawling single story home on absolute beach front, with a long white boardwalk, on the equally white sands. Master's friend I soon learned was in construction and software development. He was large and solid, not quite as tall as Master was, but a very broad and powerful looking man of about the same age. He owned this beautiful retreat by the sea amongst other properties, I believe he even had a large tract of land in Kentucky and horses. I sensed though young he had no shortage of funds at his disposal. He had a brand new truck, a gleaming white Dodge Ram 2500, unlike Master's battered old Chevy. However the best thing he owned, at least to me was a black and white Siberian husky called Devil.

I could elaborate for many paragraphs on this man and his lifestyle, but I will not tarry on the subject here. Though part of my story, it is not integral to the place I now find myself. Suffice it to say this man shared my Master's darker interests, but not with girls. He preferred boys. I do believe he had a female slave, she wore his steel collar, she was a lot older than he, dark haired and very different. I sensed I had nothing in common with her even though I was a slave. She never once spoke to me of any of her experiences or thoughts, and I kept out of her way.

I enjoyed my time here immensely. I felt privileged to live as the other half here did in Gulf Shores where every day felt like a vacation. I ran on the beach daily with Devil and although he was getting old he showed no signs of slowing down, dragging me about on his leash with wild abandon, his joy at life infectious. Each of us settled into this man's eccentric life by the beach, and Master seemed calmer and easier to be with. He went to work and I delighted in the idle life by the sea.

It was late November in the last of the fine days before winter. Not that this far south the weather ever really gets truly inclement. It was a Saturday morning Master had the day off. "Get up." He said from his comfortable place in the covers. I had been enjoying laying near him listening to the waves breaking out of the window, the smell of sea salt mingling with the fresh white sheets. I did as he said, I had learned not to tarry when he gave me a command. He obviously had plans for the day.

The house was empty but for he, Devil, and I. I made him breakfast, as for myself I had little appetite. He looked at me over the breakfast bar perched on the stool, his wild wheat colored hair touching the bench top. I know he had been thinking much of late about returning home to Denmark, he had received tragic news recently that his brother's wife had cancer and it did not look hopeful. I had begun to feel very uneasy. I had never until now thought about what might happen to me if he did choose to leave?

"Come on." He said pushing his coffee cup aside and picking up the keys to his truck. I followed him. He drove for a time in silence I had no idea where he was headed, but he often did that. He could be a man of very few words. He looked over at me as we turned up a narrow dirt track, it was so narrow the branches scraped loudly against the sides of the truck with a metallic scream. "Remember the fishing trip?" He raised his eyebrow. My mouth opened but I said naught only closing it again. How could I forget? "Today Myra we are going back to get it right." I could not believe what I had just heard him say.

I looked across at the door of the truck, the vehicle was not going very fast, perhaps I should just bail now? A few cuts and scratches but I cold run away. I felt his hand on my arm. "No Myra." He had read my thoughts precisely. We drove the final distance to the shack, it looked just as it had that hot July day. Four of his friends were there waiting. He effortlessly pulled me over the bench seat and out the drivers side door. He made no pretense at nicety. I felt like a piece of meat. I yelled for him to stop, I slapped at him, clawed at him. He merely carried me over his shoulder into the iron and wood building and commenced to bind me to the bed, The dark stain of my blood still on the mattress. He never even took all my clothes off.

I was blubbering, pleading with him, anything I could think of was tumbling out. He merely slapped me hard across the face until I desisted. "Now slave, pleasure them, and this time get it right." He snarled, settling on the chair, brawny arms crossed waiting for me to comply. His friends, some of them different from the time before used me intermittently for the entire afternoon, and until well into the night. He never touched me once, and I did not bite anyone.

It was dark, I could see the flickering light of a camp fire, the warm glow playing on the insides of the shack. I was cold and shivering I wished he would come release me, I longed for him to comfort me. He did finally, I could hear his heavy foot falls approaching, how I knew it was him I could not be sure, but I just knew. I saw his handsome visage silhouetted in the doorway, he filled the opening, standing quietly for a time. I knew better than to entreat him. He untied me in silence and carried me from the building towards the river. Heartlessly he threw me in to it's cold, muddy depths and told me to wash myself. I stood there and cried.

This is the summary, be it a lengthy one, of the main events that led up to my unerring obedience I have to this man today. Over a year later he apparently crossed the line with a young girl who did tell authorities of his behavior. I believe this incident was not an isolated one. I really did not know the full story of it and all the sordid details, but I do know Frej was tipped off he was being hunted. He decided he would embark for Denmark forthwith. Leaving me in his friend's care until such a time as he could arrange for me to join him. By the time the police questioned me I had turned eighteen and there was little they could do. I maintained my silence, in spite what most suspected I really knew. I spent my days finding in spite of his cruelty that we were indeed two of a kind. I pined for him, and dreamed of the day we could be reunited. Living my every moment in that hope...............

DENMARK

To behold him at the airport again I cannot describe, searching the sea of faces, strangers who mean nothing to me. Just those passing on their own travels in that moment. It was late, looking through the large panes of glass onto a world of dark interspersed by the glow of thousands of lights. Amber, white, and tungsten stars, in the universe of the distant city. Voices carry to my ears yet I make no sense of them, most in languages I do not understand, disembodying surreal. The architecture of this place was beautiful in it's passing simplicity, and although I took it in I was searching only for him.

I did not have long to dwell on nervous thoughts of possible abandonment in this strange, crowded setting. There he was, unmistakable, tall, handsome, and proud, my modern day barbarian. He had sighted me first, and was just as I had last remembered him. Yet after all these months to gaze on him again he was a stranger, made new again by my long isolation. I ran to him with all the abandon of a tiny child, mindless of anyone else, he was all I could see, my shining prince who had in spite of my doubts kept his promise. He had not abandoned me.

I trembled in his presence. I was lost for words. He was ever cool and stoic, and led me to the car his hand firm on my arm. In the darkness, as this day closed to midnight I did not see much of his city or his homeland. I now by agreeing to come to him, give consent to live my life cloistered within his walls. He is different now, somehow even more Masterly in his own land. I cannot explain. I am overjoyed, so glad to be by him again, yet fearful of the true Master slave experience I have come into. I know not a soul but him here, there is nowhere to run. I am at last understanding the measure of true slavery.

The journey through the darkened city streets is confusing, dissociative. I feel I do not belong here, like a fugitive escaping into a foreign land, a spy perhaps. I set my eyes on sights that are unfamiliar to me and I wonder if they shall ever become so? He does not speak to me of any more than cursory pleasantries, how was the flight, and of course the mandatory did I miss him?

The car stops, he has parked it in the street. His home is as unremarkable as the next. Single story and small, clad in dull brown brick. I get out and take one long look at it, the air is cold and I can see my breath hanging in the still night air. I shiver and pull my thin sweater tighter about me, sincerely hoping it will be warmer inside. He retrieves my suitcase lifting it as though it is little more than an overnight bag. In it is contained the sum of my entire world, my memories, my few precious treasures. I feel his arm on my back guiding me to the door, the street lights harsh on his face in the otherwise darkness.

He fumbles with the key in the lock, and the door opens inward, slowly. His hand again urges me forward, his warm bulk behind me. I feel the warm air, his home smells of him, and stale cigarettes. Yet he does not smoke. I take in the front room for the first time as he flicks on the lamp, it's soft yellow glow flattering to his very unkempt abode. He does not comment on this, but I sense he can tell what I am thinking as I analyze his private world. I gaze on his eclectic belongings discarded where he has last had use of them. The old mismatched furnishings, and the items leaning against the walls. I can see he has little time for, or pride in his home. He stands close behind me I can feel his urgency, his unparalleled need, and without further ceremony he takes me where I stand...............

SEEDS OF BETRAYAL

I grow used to his home and what is required of me. I have questions burning inside, so many questions, but I choose to ask very few of those. The passage of time will be my teacher. Yet I am ill prepared for the loneliness that burns within, is this what solitary inmates feel? To that end I have decided though it is a risky undertaking and fraught with danger, to use his computer, to connect to the outside world. Whatever the consequence.

To that end I decided to rekindle a profile page on a popular BD/SM web site. I had discovered it one day quite by accident as I surfed the internet in my closing days of living in sunny Gulf Shores, deciding to try it. I felt guilty and furtive and even though I was in the care of Master's friend I kept a profile but briefly, deleting it out of fear. It is a large heavily used site and best of all free.

Like a child drawn to candy here I sit, back at it again. I risk my Master's wrath being on there to socialize, but most importantly it is a place to pour out my feelings and emotions, and make sense of the situation I now find myself.

The computer in its dull gray case, my only contact with the outside world at this time. I sit here during the day, at least I know I am unobserved. I'm going to keep a journal of my experiences here. Master works in construction, he rises early and comes home late. I'm not a fan of this, but it is what he has done and his father and grandfather before him. So who am I to judge? I do miss the free life of the beach and my Master's friends husky, life here is cold and very different. Master has bid me to be my best for him on his return he says he has something special. My heart skips when he says this, I'm not sure if I will like it or not. I never am with him.

THE VALENTINE'S GIFT

I heard the sound of his car in the lane way and knelt naked by the front door as I have always done. It was very late. I was tired but excited, and as always joyous to see him. As he entered I did not look up. I shivered with the cold breeze that came through the doorway as it hit my skin. As he stood in front of me all I had in my sights was his battered steel toed work boots. "I do hope you have been a good girl?" I know he was looking about the room to see if I had accomplished all my cleaning.

"Yes," I all but whispered to his boots.

"I have something for you." He said, devilment in his voice. I looked up to see a large box in bright paper in his strong hands, he handed it to me. It's contents were rather weighty and I puzzled at what it might be? Master rarely bought me gifts, but when he did it always filled me with joy.

"Open it." He urged. I fumbled at the paper not wanting to tear it, he stood with his brawny arms crossed as he waited for me to comply. The item emerged from the box with a loud metallic clunk. I sat there dumbfounded, as a low chuckle emanated from Master's chest above me. I felt his hand caress my face taking hold of me under my chin and forcing me to look into his emerald green eyes. "Until now you have only played at slave?" I shivered at the menace in his voice. "Now it's time to really become one." I wanted to say no. I wanted to tear my eyes away from his, but he held me firm his jagged torn nails biting into my face. "Lets put it on shall we." His voice caressed. He let go of my face my eyes going back to the floor and the awful device that lie there.

I could not help myself. "But you know I don't want anyone else but you?" I stammered pathetically. Trying to feebly save myself from having to wear that horrible device, even in fun.

"YOU WILL DO AS YOU ARE TOLD!" He snapped. I had not heard him talk to me like this for a long time, not since the long ago cutting incident. Tears were already running down my cheeks, this was not at all what I had expected, nor wanted either. He was oblivious, pulling me to my feet and fitting the awful metal chastity device. I winced as he pushed the plug into me, and in no time at all he had the cold uncomfortable thing tight on me and locked fast. "It looks good on you." He commented appreciatively, a sly grin on his rough features was all I could see through the curtain of tears. He left me there to change his clothes and take a shower. We usually shower together, but he did not question my absence. When he returned I was still where he had left me. I do not know how I will wear this thing? Surely he does not really mean me to wear this all day while he is gone?

I wanted to question his decision but did not dare. He kindly told me that as I was now alone and no longer in the care of his best friend it was most necessary. I wanted to argue otherwise but I could see the look on his face and knew it was not wise.

The dildo inside me made me want to scream to have him in me, I guess that was the purpose of it. Still I would have wanted him anytime of the day anyway. There were so many questions I wanted to ask, like how easy would it even be to go to the toilet? I'm not sure I liked the way this was going at this point. I really wanted to be home, by the beach. Anywhere but here.

He did not remove the horrid object as the evening wore on, and did not choose to give me any sexual relief. He made me pleasure him orally and I got nothing in return, then as it was late he lay down holding me possessively in his bed. I could tell it was going to be a hell of a weekend.

I cried most of that weekend whilst I did my chores. I don't know what to feel? He knows I love him and I am devoted only to him, it was he who insisted I be shared. It was never my desire or wish. We did not do what we usually did in times past, it was like this weekend set a new precedence for something else. Something I really don't understand. What makes a man so possessive? Honestly he's so good looking he could have anyone, why do this to me? I'm angry right now and confused, and desiring so much to leave, but there is nowhere to leave to. He is silent towards me, contemptuous even, or is it just cruelty? I can sense this in the set of his body and his sarcastic choice of his few well placed words. All I can think of is this horrid steel object, and it would not be half so bad if it did not have the plug in it.

Sunday night I finally broke down and cried at his feet, begging for him to reconsider. He sat bare chested in the large shabby leather chair as is his usual place in the evenings, looking down on me like some Viking lord. For a long time he just studied me in my grief, listening I hoped to my pleas. He just smiled saying nothing and turned on the television. He has always been a hard emotionless wall of a man all the years I have known him. Even when we first met he was cold and detached, something drew me to him even at my tender age of self discovery, and yet something else told me to flee. Maybe I should have listened to it, but here I am and my choices are very much diminished. For the first time I realized submission to him was not a game, and I felt the cold chill of this realization wash over me, sickening me to the pit of my stomach. So many questions I have and I am too afraid to ask them of him.

Its was very late before he decided to rouse himself from his chair. He works very hard during the week physically and on the weekends he loves to sleep late and do very little. I jumped at the touch of his large warm hand on my shoulder as I sat abjectly on the floor wrapped in nothing but a blanket lost in my disturbing thoughts. "Come." Was all he said going into the bathroom.

I shook myself of my stupor realizing he was wanting a bath, and it was my duty to ready it for him. I raced ahead of him while he casually undressed, looking at his finely muscled body out of the corner of my eye as I set about pleasing him by doing this duty. I have always thought of him as a modern day barbarian, he does not behave like so many other men I have known. He sees, he takes, by open avarice or stealth if need be. Just like he took me, when I was not remotely ready. It mattered not to him, he saw and he wanted that was all he cared. I wondered fleetingly while the tub was filling if I would meet his family soon? I hoped so but as yet no word.

I was again drawn out of my reverie by the touch of his hand at my waist and I was overjoyed to see he was releasing me from the dreaded steel belt. It had marked indention's into my skin, the awful unforgiving steel I so hated, at last removed. I had already decided I would do anything not to have it on again. He smiled at the way I looked at him, the kind of smile that never reaches his eyes, and I felt afraid.

He lowered himself into the bath, the hot water almost spilling out the sides as he is a big man, and motioned me to join him. He is well over double my size and I climbed in to sit straddled on his hard belly. That was not all that was hard and he pushed himself inside me without any ceremony. After two days of the awful belt and the dildo the need I felt was unashamed, and I fucked him with wild abandon I do not think I have ever felt in all my life. Though as was usual the moment was often spoiled by the pain of the badly healed cut he had given me for refusing to pleasure his friends such a long time ago. I tried to concentrate on something else and will the dull pain away that often sought to spoil my pleasure. I could see he had noticed, he just lay back and smiled one of his cruel sardonic smiles until he chose to cum.

Master's house is old and not particularly modern, the bathroom is an awful sickly green tile with dirty grout one can never clean, trust me I've tried. The tub of all things is pink, I like pink but it all looks so dreary and old. His home is nothing like his friend's beach house in Alabama. All windows, sea front views of white and blue, beautiful furnishings, and the latest appointments. Master seems not to care that his house is little more than a trog den and it depresses me, especially the nasty basement.

After we dried off and I combed the tangles from his long mane of mid back length, wheat colored hair, admiring his huge shoulders and strong arms. I figured the object of my horror was forgotten, but no I was mistaken. He saw me freeze and make to run from him, catching me by the hair. Sometimes short hair might be a good thing I mused, and running in a small house decidedly foolish. "Oh no." He said, "It's going back on." Before I could think better, aroused by my dread of the past few days my mouth had already betrayed me.

"No, I can't take it again, please? You know I will never do anything with anyone." I entreated, talking too fast, his big hand twisting my hair making me wince. There was no reply just a stinging open handed slap to the side of my face. It was so hard I could only open my mouth to gasp in pain. I had said the forbidden word to him, no. Before I knew it he put the thing back on, and even though I had no words I was grateful he had at least not used the plug.

"Get used to it it's going to be on all week." He saw me slump with resignation quite defeated. He defeats me easily. I guess I should be ashamed but in reality I have set myself into this position. I cannot blame anyone else.

I lay silent and awake listening to the traffic wondering at the strange and new unseen world I now occupy? As yet no one knows I even exist. Terror tugs at me in the dark I no longer feel so brave. It occurs to me that if he wished he could merely snuff out my insignificant life and no one would be the wiser. My disjointed family would never inquire, let alone search. As far as they are concerned I have done well. Silent tears run down my cheeks wetting the pillow, as I gaze at the patterns of the car lights on the window. I think I now truly understand the immensity of 24/7 slavery. This is real, no longer the pretend game of my early teens.

Master is at work, and again I sneak to the computer. It is his computer, as everything here is. All unfamiliar to me. I feel scared to use it but I do realize he is not at all computer savvy. I probably know more about it than he does. It's not a very good machine but it still connects me to the outside world. In a way I can be bolder here as his friend who was good with computers is not present. He would have discovered my internet tryst for sure. I don't know what would happen if I got caught? It makes my heart beat very fast just sitting here as I know its a forbidden activity. I so want to connect with others like myself and detail my voyage into 24/7 for all to read. I guess it is also a way to fill my long days, there are only so many times

I can tidy the house. This little forbidden journal will be my solace.

The weekday evenings seem to be most predictable with us. Master's car rumbles up the adjoining lane way and I kneel naked at the door waiting his presence. Sometimes he is early, sometimes he is very late. He tells me not where he has been and I know better than to ask. I hate the cold here I seem to feel it intensely. Snow on the windows is novel but I am not so sure I will ever enjoy the cold weather. I have not left the house since my arrival its been two weeks now. In this place it seems easy to lose grasp of time. I want to speak of it to Master yet the words die in my mouth before I can even utter the first one.

I find I spend dinner silent, serving him. He likes red meat, he seems to be happy to eat it every day. He loves plain food, I am not so fond of it and crave something with more taste. As a result I find I have little appetite, not that I really eat a lot anyway. I chew on my bread and decide to frame my question. It takes great courage. I try to disarm him by giving him one of my more flirtatious looks. I see he responds and I draw my tiny vestige of courage from it.

"I've been here a while now Sir. Are you going to show me around......outside?" It sounded lame but it was the best I could muster. A cruel smile twisted his ruggedly handsome face as he locked his vibrant green eyes on mine. Looking all the primal savage through his mane of rampant golden hair, crouched over his partially eaten meal like a possessive lion. I had to look away, as his eyes bored into mine cold and heartless.

"You my dear." He put bold emphasis in the word dear. "Are not ready." Still I was not done, looking at the floor I perilously continued.

"I want to see your home town, and when will I meet your family? You said............"

He laughed loudly it was a guttural belly laugh, pulling the rest of my speech up flat. I just looked across the table at him, not at his face but at his partly unbuttoned shirt. He rose from the table, for a large man he could be very agile. I quailed in fear as he reached my side waiting for some form of retribution. However there was none, he just stood there on the periphery of my vision. I felt the warmth of his body close to me and his hand gently stroking my hair.

"Ah little Myra." He said somewhat fondly. "You have much to learn, you think you are my slave but in reality you have barely started on the path. Until now its just been nothing more than games." I baulked at this, I did not feel anything we had done was merely a game. I'm sure he felt me stiffen underneath his broad hand. If he did he did not show he had. I looked down miserably at my mostly uneaten plate. The hand resumed petting me. "You will learn to be patient, and you will learn not to question me. I know what is best for you Myra, even when you can't see it." I hung my head in resignation, he was the most impossible man to talk to, or reason with. There was nothing more to be said.

So this house was to be my entire world for the time being, only my adherence to his edict to keep me from straying from beyond it's bounds. I mulled this over as I cleaned up the remnants of dinner, Master had already removed himself to the lounge room. I was glad to just be alone with my thoughts over the dishes. These simple daily tasks in some way although mundane gave me some kind of solace, just like they had done while my parents fought in the other room when I was no more than a little girl.

I went down stairs to the basement to do the washing. I did not like it there. I do not like basements at all and this one is damper and more dreary than most. The house is old and this airless, light less space gouged out of the earth, is some place I never wish to be, it seems everything that comes to rest here falls into decay. There is no other appropriate place for the washer and dryer so I must frequent here. Every time I come down here I feel like I cannot breathe, and I feel dirty as well. I fear Master imprisoning me in here, but I would never let on my fear lest he use it. I now realize I must walk a careful line and not tell him the things I find I cannot bear, lest they be turned against me.

The evening was uneventful, Master sat in his big overstuffed chair flicking through the channels on the television. I sat at his feet, quiet and introspective wishing I had a cat or a puppy. He did not converse with me at all, it was like I was not there. Much later he took me to his bed. I was glad to be freed of the chastity belt and he made gentle love to me. I let him do as he wished, I do like it when he is this way inclined with me. I decided to use the moment to broach something I needed to understand.

"Master?" He looked at me but did not stop me uttering my question. "Tell me, why do I really need to even wear this terrible belt?" He was quiet for a while. I lay next to him against his hard body, my head cradled beneath his arm.

"You can't see it can you Myra?" I shook my head in answer. He sighed, shifted his position a little and continued. "I see the way other men look at you, they would if they could, have you in a heartbeat." I was not so sure of this, but I did recall many times I had to extricate myself from many over eager boys, whom I did not want the attentions of. Maybe he was right, at least a little? Still this seemed somewhat extreme.

"You are mine, inside and out, all of you." His arm tightened around me. I felt myself tingle at his words, his possession was so thorough, it always had been. I cannot imagine what he would have done if I had have been with another man. I imagine it would not have been pretty. However in all honesty even if he never believed me, I was his, and only his. I did not need a piece of steel to prove it. Sadly he believed I did.

"It annoys me." I whined. "I really don't need it, I'm here alone, no one comes here......."

"Myra." He growled. I knew better than to continue. The argument was closed, and he rolled over and went to sleep leaving me to stare at his great back.

The day starts in the same way every day during the week just before dawn. I feel Master stir and he places his hand on the top of my head. The unspoken command for me to pleasure him beneath the covers with my mouth. He rarely cums I'm not sure if its my failing or his control, but he lays there eyes closed his large arms behind his head propped on the pillow. He sometimes pats me gently on my head while I do this, though he never speaks. The alarm finally breaks the quiet of the early morning and begrudgingly he leaves the bed.

He is always grumpy in the morning and I tend to avoid him while he wakes up. Easily done as I hurry to make breakfast. He sits and eats and does not converse with me, sometimes I try to lighten his mood, and some days I know not to try. Today was one of those days, he is a man of few words. Then he is heading for the door, I glimpse the street and the rows of tightly positioned old houses that line it. Briefly I wonder at the people who live in them and what their lives are like? He pauses by the door and says as he does each day. "Be good." I know he means it. My day alone begins............

I am often startled by the mail man, as the mail for the day comes sailing through the door to alight on the carpet. Each time I die a thousand deaths, yet I know it's is not Master for I did not hear his car nor the key grate in the door lock. Still my nerves and my guilt get the better of me. Today a package arrived it was just large enough to fit through the mail slot and it fell with a thud to the floor. Its silly but after days in this tiny insular world I have become a lot braver and more curious as to the goings on in Master's life. I find I like to examine his mail. Most of it seems quite ordinary, and of course I have next to no grasp on the language either. This does not help my thirst for discovery. I removed the package from the floor it's contents were quite weighty for it's size. Even in shipping I could see the corners had been crushed by it's weight. I shook it, it was packed well and did not yield any clues to it's contents. Now it seems I have something to ponder on all day.

COLLAR OF STEEL

Master was home early this day, why I do not know, and he really caught me by surprise. I knew when he sighted the box it had been something he had been waiting for. He placed it on the computer desk which I had hurriedly vacated only moments before, not expecting his early return. I hope he did not sense my panic as I knelt on the floor naked as I always did, eyes to the floor, heart hammering. Fortunately he paid me little heed and leisurely opened his mail. He had his back to me, I could smell the male scent of him emanating from his sweaty work clothes. I can never understand it but the combination of my fear and his presence somehow arouses me more than anything on earth. I spend my time studying the floor and glancing at him when I dare through my hair, calming my panic at nearly being caught. He does not open the package like I assumed he would but instead leaves it on the desk. He turns in the chair to look at me. "Herover." I pause at his simple request, my mind trying to process the word. I notice he now lapses into his native tongue more here, but I guess he speaks it all day. After all English is his second language.

He sits me on his lap, when he does this I feel like a small child, seeking love I never had from my hard, distant, father, who thought daughters were a burden and a waste of his time. I am intoxicated by his closeness, these moments for me make any perceived hardship worth while. He places his broad hand in the centre of my chest, his jade eyes locking on to mine, and his eyes narrow. His stare is very intense I feel he lays bare my motives, my innermost feelings all exposed for him to see plainly. My heart is still beating wildly and I am not sure the actress is good enough to mask my fear of coming so close to being caught at my Internet tryst. He smiles, he can have a beautiful smile, but his smile is not one of happiness, it is one of self satisfaction. I am sure he senses I have been up to some mischief, I wait for the accusation. I have learned silence is my best friend. He looks around the room, I try not to swallow, but he feels it and looks at me again. I know he is looking for anything out of place.

Thankfully he lapses back to English. "I have something for you." He removes his hand from its place over my rapid heart, twisting his body to reach the parcel on the desk. He tears it open, I notice the dirt under all his nails, and abrasions on his hands. "I promised you this for a long time. It is a Turian slave collar. I know you will not understand it's meaning, but it does not matter." He held up the stainless steel circlet, it was smooth and cold to the touch as he opened it and placed it about my neck. It fit perfectly, and felt heavy, somehow fitting, adding to the mantle of slavery I felt I already carried. I put my hand to my neck the collar was hard and inflexible, just as he is and his rules. He was not finished, producing two matching bracelets which he perfunctorily affixed to each wrist, testing to see if it was possible for me to slide them off. Satisfied, he just sat long moments with me in his lap, examining me closely. Talking in his native language to me softly. I had no idea what it was he said, but it was in it's self very beautiful.

I've never met a man like Master, one moment he is the gentle rolling sea, the next he is a raging storm. I am not sure if he was just sitting there enjoying me, or perhaps dwelling on how he would deal with what he had sensed was a mischief. Abruptly he stood holding me to him, the room was beginning to darken and there was no illumination. "So tell me why were you so panicked today?" I held his gaze in a brave attempt at bluff, thankful the room was getting dark. I had no idea how to answer or even construct a lie. However I couldn't deny it either, I was trapped. I did not answer, I could say nothing in my defense. I could only hope he would not press me too hard. He stood before me patiently awaiting an answer, but my mind was devoid of any words. I was not even in the possession of a feeble excuse that seemed suitable as a cover up. "Very well." He said. "I will beat it out of you."

I panicked and pulled away from him, he slapped me hard and I fell to the floor narrowly missing the sharp edge of the coffee table. He grabbed me by the collar and hauled me to my feet. Already I could see though it looked like jewelry and would arouse little attention if worn in public, it had a very practical side.

He took me into the bedroom removing my chastity belt, pushing me face down on the bed. He proceeded to tie me with rope across the bed to the metal frame. I already knew what was coming. I kept saying no and begging him to stop. He was not moved by my pleas. He sensed something amiss and he wanted to know what it was. Secrets of any kind were forbidden in his world. Master is passionate but he is also careful, once he had me tied the way he wanted me he gagged me with his clothes. It was suffocating and I could not utter any more than muffled sounds. No one would hear me at all, Master had always been careful about that. He took off his belt and I had no choice but to take his hiding. I was glad I could not speak. I am sure I would have confessed, but then he could not afford anyone to hear me either, so I had already won.

I lost track of the strokes, my father would hit us this way when I was a little girl. Once I remember he cut my brother with his belt buckle badly, and blood went everywhere. I hate pain it both scares and angers me. My behind and the back of my legs were red and burning when he did finally stop. The room was now dark, I heard him unzip his jeans, he pulled my hair back holding it in one fist as he fucked me hard. He came very swiftly, I could feel him spasm inside of me his breathing rapid. Just as swiftly he was done and left the room.

I could hear him in the bathroom taking a shower, the sound of the running water lulling me to calmness after the adrenaline left my body. At some point I must have slept and woke much later. He was in the kitchen making coffee, a look at the bedside clock revealed it was nine-thirty. I so wanted to move, but it was impossible. My knees hurt on the hard floor, my lower thighs still secured to the bed, my wrists pulling against the steel bracelets, and the gag soaked in my saliva. I sighed too exhausted to cry.

He must have heard me, he does not miss much. He entered the dark room, he did not put on the light as he unbound me, my mouth was dry and sore from the gag. He carried me to the other room, thankfully only the lamp was on, and the curtains were drawn. Even this dim yellow light hurt my eyes, but not half as much as my rear end was hurting. He took me to the lounge and placed me on it throwing a blanket over me. I winced as he set me down. He sat close and made me drink some water. I was still fearful he would continue his interrogation. When he did finally speak I thought I would die.

"Myra, you silly girl." He admonished. "I cannot believe you would have taken that over such a small thing?" I sat silent hurting and confused, I could not understand what he was speaking of. "It was only a dish." He went on shaking his shaggy blonde head in disbelief, and I realized earlier that day I had broken a plate still fumbling with the newness of his kitchen. I began to cry, the small sobs mounting to very loud wailing, in my relief he had believed I was afraid because I had broken a plate. Oh I had been saved, and I howled unrestrained tears of relief until I fell asleep on him.

Its been a tough week for me I have had hours alone to question the things that are happening to me. The reality of being a slave is a difficult thing to encompass. It seemed easier to be one in my own country than here in my Master's homeland. It's a very disembodying experience. I'm no one here to anyone. I exist only for him and his desires. Its a dark thing in reality, and I now wonder how many really do it? I suspect not too many.

I'm stiff and sore today, he still stubbornly insisted on putting on the chastity belt before he departed further enhancing my pain. Sitting down has to be accomplished with great care. This morning though before he left for work I was happy to hear his brother who he has told me much about would be visiting this Friday evening. I'm heartened to at least be getting the chance to know and meet with some of Master's family. Perhaps once I meet them I will feel more part of things here?

Reminders of Master are at every turn, the steel on my body. His scent in the bed and on his clothes that lay heaped in profusion over the chairs and on the floor. He is a very untidy man. I have often been guilty of holding them to me sometimes during his long absences, breathing him in. His stubble rakes the sink, his golden hair on the bathroom tiles. Yes, he is everywhere watching even when he is not present.

SVEND

This evening I so desire to leave a good impression. I was very curious and a little nervous to be meeting Master's big brother. He often spoke of him and it appeared they are very close even if he is much older than my Master is.

It felt most strange to greet my Master at the door fully dressed and standing. The unforgiving steel beneath my clothing, about my neck and wrists made me never forget what I really was to him. Master caught my eye with his own intense ones, and I could see the small knowing hint of a smile forming, as he saw my discomfort and took his delight in it. His brother was every bit as handsome as Master, aged somewhere in his late thirties, with gray eyes the color of an encroaching storm, and the same full head of long hair. He had a neatly trimmed goatee and a few tattoos, unlike Master's skin which is clean, but other than that he was Master in every way, yet older. Unmistakably brothers for all the world to see.

I smiled and greeted him nervously with my stumbling words. I have always been painfully shy and much prefer to just stand back and not be noticed in any social encounter. He seemed pleasant enough, his English nowhere near as accomplished as my Master, and his accent heavy in his words. He was a little hard to understand. Something about him bothered me. I cannot say what. Though I did realize they had both been drinking, not enough to be drunk, but enough to get them in a buoyant mood. Maybe that was all I was detecting?

Introductions over I served the meal. The two men obviously had much catching up to do, and they spoke animatedly in a mixture of English and Danish. I assume they only used the English for the things they wished me to be privy to. I did not have much to contribute in the company of these two handsome and charismatic men. I spent most of dinner avoiding their eyes and shifting on my chair minimizing the pain in my behind, and was only too happy to retreat to the solace of the kitchen to do the dishes.

Lost in the patterns the soap suds made floating on the water in the sink I jumped with a start to hear Master calling me. I had hoped I had been quite forgotten. I hurried to the lounge room to see what he wanted, I should have known, drinks. I hurried back to the kitchen to get his favorite, Schnapps. I returned swiftly.

"Put those down Myra." He indicated the coffee table, and I set down the tray the little glasses clattering into one another, loud in the quiet room. "Now Myra, show my dear brother what you really are to me?" I balked at his words, assuring myself I had misheard him. I stood motionless and silent, my heart thumping in my chest. He could do this to me so swiftly and I hated myself for it. "Take your clothes off slave." He ordered, in his usual hard edged tone. I could all but taste the threat in it. The worse thing was his brother did not seem at all shocked and I realized stupidly he must have been in on this the whole time. I quailed at his command.

Master looked at his elder brother apologetically. "She's a little slow, and way too shy." At once leaving his place on the lounge to help me do as he commanded. I thought he would hit me. He all but tore my top off pinching my nipples hard, as he did so sending shameful feelings to places deep inside. I felt so ashamed as my clothes lay crumpled on the threadbare carpet, along with my pride. My face flushed and red for all to witness. I hung my head and stared dumbly at the floor while the two men appraised me like I was some witless animal.

My mind flashing back to the group of Master's friends who had shared me in a similar fashion long years before in the river shack. Tonight here it was happening again. I wanted to die of my shame. The only positive was he saw fit to remove the belt.

"Drinks slave." Master pushed me to the coffee table with the back of his hand as he resumed his place. I wanted to run, I wanted to hide, he knew it, I knew it. In this dangerous game we played. Knowing any moment I might break and run to the police, condemning him to all hell, and he prepared at any point to do anything in his power to prevent me. However my thoughts remained, just thoughts, I felt nothing but numb with the shame of the moment trying to concentrate on pouring the drinks. I assumed correctly, fortunately, to serve Master's brother first. I could not look at him though I could feel his eyes on me, his calloused hand touched mine as he took the glass, I jumped. Master laughed and I felt a new wave of heat flush my cheeks. I took the other glass to Master but he did not take it and made me stand before him for long awkward moments.

"Stand straight." He ordered in a tone dripping velvet, his voice thick with arousal. "Don't spill any." He pushed his fingers deep inside of me, it was all I could do to stop my knees caving in under me. My body reacting on it's own volition to his invasion, my eyes not on him but on the rim of the glass in my every effort not to spill a drop. I felt I stood there inert for the longest time, yet I know in reality it was not that long before he took the glass and I was forgotten at his feet on the floor. The men resumed their conversation in Danish, I used to so love to hear Master speak in his exotic tongue, but on this night it chilled me with unspeakable fear. I knew I was the subject of much it, and tried to blot it out gazing at the television that lent it's ambiance to the background, wishing I had the distraction of a kitten or a puppy.

The clock was way past midnight edging toward one before the men stirred, and the alcohol bottle empty. I rose from the floor as I sensed Master wished to retire for the evening. His hand went to my arm, and before I knew it he pushed me toward his brother and left the room.

I felt as though the entire room had collapsed inward crushing me. I felt his brother's arm encircle me and guide me to the spare room. I knew better than to make a scene. I had traveled this road with Master before and could expect no quarter. In a fleeting thought I dwelt on the past and on the many conversations we had had on lack of choice. Tonight I was seeing the merit of the lesson driven home, yes lack of choice, the life of a real slave.

The spare room smelt of disuse like many such rooms do, and it was decidedly cool within. Life was becoming surreal. Here I was in the arms of a man who was to me a complete stranger, yet in the darkness possessed many of the familiarities of the man I knew all too well. That frightening man who pushed my boundaries, and could crush my world with just a glance. It was the weirdest thing. I let him do as he pleased, he was not cruel, he was most gentle. He did not talk nor did he belittle me in any fashion. He lingered over me a long time in the thin light that spilled through the window. I did not like the fact he kissed me deeply but again I did not fight him. Kissing to me is an act of sincere love only, and he cheapened this for me. After he had sated his desire he sent me from the warmth of his bed, back to my Master.

I lingered at the window pane in the lounge room tracing lines on the gelid glass, watching the street lights and those of the occasional passing car. It was well after three am, the city was quiet, and I felt like the only sleepless one in the world. I toyed with the prospect of throwing on a large overcoat and running into the street, and far away. However I knew I would not really do it. It was my mind unwilling to face new things, and it was playing tricks on me, that was all. He was my Master and he had not hurt me, he had only injured only my pride.

I climbed into bed beside him, his brother's semen still sticky on my thighs, I felt soiled and cried into the pillow trying to be a silent as possible. Master was not asleep I realized with a start as he turned to face me and lick my tears from my face. He held me tightly to him and whispered in my ear nothing more than. "Brother's share." I knew this would not be the last.

Saturday morning was most difficult. I was tired as I had lain awake most of the remainder of that night my mind in such turmoil I could not find the solace of sleep. The men slept late but I did not, rousing myself to prowl the small house and finally make breakfast when I was sure they would finally stir.

Master entered the kitchen kissing me and cheerful, as though nothing untoward had happened, and I believe in his mind it had not. I did my best to keep his good humor even if I did not feel it myself. He sidled up to me and said hoarsely. "I'm glad you were a good girl Myra. You gave my brother a great gift, his wife died a few months back." I shivered, the skin on the back of my neck prickling. He knew he was doing this to me, he never missed a thing when it came to my feelings. He fed on them, my fear, and discomfort. "Perhaps if you continue to be good I might get you that kitten?" I looked at him. Longing to have something living and warm to spend my long, lonely days with.

"You will?" I questioned tenuously.

"I just might." Was all he said. Even in darkness I realized there could always be found a ray of light, and I clung to the thought.

The time he spends at home on the weekends seems fleeting, even if at times it proves testing. As this last weekend had been. I was relieved to see his brother depart Saturday, but I just know that will not be an isolated event. Master and I did not speak of it, I wanted to but deep inside I did not really wish to hear his answers. Instinctively I knew them already, perhaps this is why women are gifted with intuition, it's a survival skill.

Again it is Monday and I sit here at the computer, my solace and my dark secret in its gray case beneath the old desk. With my couple of hours to write, talk with others, and dream.

THE KITTEN AND THE TRUTH

I called her Cleo, Master brought her home in a cat carrier, he said he had rescued her from a shelter. He commented she was a cat in a cage just like I was, and I guess he was right. She was a tiny cat, half grown, soft gray and white, with medium length fur that felt like the softest down. I loved her instantly and she loved me too. Looking up at me with her pretty gold, green eyes, trusting, loving, and promising me many hours of solace and companionship.

"Now remember." He warned. "It's is not to ruin anything or it's is gone." I nodded holding the squirming, purring, bundle close. Sensing the finality in his voice. He did not seem the kind to have much patience for pets, come to think of it he never really showed any interest or affection toward his friend's dog either when we lived in Alabama.

I had wanted a pet, especially a kitten for my entire life, and it was all too easy for Cleo to become a large focus for me. I tended to her care diligently, mindful though her needs never got in the way of Master's. He was first and foremost, there could be no exception to this.

Understandably I was so happy that evening and stupidly I let my guard down. The question was simple in its self, and not meant to be threatening in any way. I did not expect the rather adverse reaction Master had over it though. All I asked was when were we going to see his mother and father? He grabbed me quick as a cat. I jumped dropping a coffee cup, it shattered in many pieces on the floor.

"Myra." He growled. I was confused, what I had done to make him suddenly so angry. His fingers were pressing hard into my upper arm. He dragged me to the kitchen chair which he sat in, pulling me on to his lap, holding my face in both hands so close to his own. I could not pull away and did not try though he was hurting, the strength in his hands was phenomenal. Behind me the tap dripped into the cold dishwater, and the television droned on in the other room to an empty audience. He took a breath I sensed he was about to say something profound, something I did not wish to hear.

"You Myra are a slave, you are NOT a lover, you are NOT my wife, you are NOT my friend." The words were almost whispered, quietly powerful. My head reeled. I did not like where this was going. "I intend..............." He paused for a long time, I could barely breathe. I could tell he was trying to frame his words carefully, and not let his rash anger control what he really needed to say. "Remember the things we spoke about, about ownership, about being a slave?" I nodded with the minimal movement he allowed me. I could feel his hardness as I sat on his lap even through the rough fabric of his jeans. My betraying tears were already beginning to run and again I could see though impassioned, he was enjoying this. "You are a slave, you will not be meeting my family, only my brother knows you are here, and he is not going to be telling anyone. You will not be leaving this house, or my world, you are here Myra to exist only for ME."

"But you said.........." I countered feebly. He snarled at me like a rabid dog.

"What I said back in the USA and what I do now Myra are completely different things." He sniggered, enjoying my defeat. I looked down at the space between our bodies at his navel, eyes clouded with tears.

"You're mine Myra." He reiterated. "Now you have been a good girl." He went on. "That's why you still have free run of the house in my absence. But mark my words if I even suspect you trying to leave, or contacting anyone, I will lock you up." He pulled my hair and made me look at him. I felt he could see the contents of my soul, I was wet with my fear and ashamed all at the same time. "But so far so good." He said, seemingly satisfied, pushing me off him as he rose. "Now clean that up." With that he retreated to his chair and the news.

It was the next day I realized the phone had been removed, the small side table bereft of it's constant companion, only it's dusty outline remained to assure me it had even existed. I rushed to the computer, as always it seemed to take forever to turn on. I sat patiently staring at the start up screen, but no to my relief the internet had either been overlooked, or for reasons of his own Master did not see fit to remove this life line to the rest of the world. I sat for long moments feeling like a participant in a game of Russian roulette, was it a trap, or merely he did not feel the presence of this service a threat? Finally my desire to talk to others won out, and I sat feeling like some front line journalist in a war torn country desperately trying to get my story through, in spite of the inherent dangers. Cleo on my lap oblivious to my mission.

It's Friday again and as usual I have the day on my own. Cleo makes me so happy with her cute antics and her loving nature she is already proving to be the light of my life. I do not feel nearly as lonely as I used to while Master is away. I so treasure her. I get most of my duties done now quite swiftly as I am beginning to really settle in to Master's home. In my free time I attempt daily to learn all I can of his language via the internet. It seems I have a long road ahead, but some words are beginning to stick. The mail drops through the door and nothing has my name on it. It's very disembodying for me, not that I ever received an abundance of mail. However to get nothing, not a single thing, feels very odd, like I have been completely banished from existence. I guess in a way I have.

I AM NOT THE FIRST

I was so upset and shaken last Friday I could not bring myself to write of my discovery.................

I was scouring the spare room for some reading when I came on some old photo albums. They were right at the bottom of the book shelf, dusty and forgotten. I took them to the light of the window and sat on the corner of the bed. I spent a long time engrossed in their faded contents, there it was a complete encapsulation of my Master's often mysterious history. Photos of his childhood, his big brother, and his mother and father who I still hoped he would someday let me meet. I could see plainly Master got his size from his father, but his handsomeness came from his mother. She had been very beautiful indeed.

As I flicked through the pages I watched him grow from the blonde cheeky boy, to the angular teenager, and into the man he was today. As he aged there were many unidentified people in the pictures, I wondered who they all were knowing I would never directly ask him. My fertile imagination running wild. There was one nameless person who captivated me and I burned to know just who she was? She was slim, dark and young, with full lips and a thick mane of dark burgundy hair. Her eyes haunted me in every photo, and to me she looked sad, somehow betrayed.

I closed the book, and got down on the floor to put them away, but they did not want to return to their tight place in the base of the book shelf. Cleo was not helping me either by clamoring into the unoccupied space. I then realized there were some CD's that had fallen down, preventing them from doing so. I pulled them out they had nothing written on them, perhaps they were music or something? I replaced the albums and went to the computer to investigate. To my delight they were not music at all but some more modern photographs. I flicked through them stopping at some, skipping swiftly through others, while I drank my tea. I was greatly enjoying my find and learning about Master's past. Until I opened the folder with the pictures of the sad girl that is. I stared at the disturbing images on the screen my hand to my mouth in silent shock. I realized I was not the first.

My good sense told me not to delve further but the damage was done, the files were dated 2004. This was before we had met, who was she, where was she now? Of more importance to me was, did he still see her? I felt ill in the pit of my stomach and a cold sweat crept over me, but I could not tear my eyes away from the photos of her naked flesh. The tattoo of the little sun on her lower belly in black, and her haunting eyes. She never looked anything but sad and vulnerable, and in some of the pictures she looked deathly afraid crouching on the floor smeared in what I presumed was her own blood.

If I wanted to doubt what I was looking at I could not, some of the pictures had been taken in this very house. I could not refute that. Master was clearly in some of the pictures as were other men; men I did not know. I found I had to look at them all in my morbid fascination, wondering if he would hurt me like that, who did she belong to, did she want what they had done? So many questions.

The weekend was routine and the two of us spent it alone. I must confess I looked at him a lot differently than I had before. Perhaps he is a scary predator, the lion in the grass, and I the gazelle? I wondered incessantly about the girl?

Many nights I lie sleepless as I did this one past, twisting the slave steel about my neck. It rests heavy on my collar bone and my desires and fears rest heavy on my heart and mind. Life with Master is falling into a pattern, he uses me before he sleeps and even though sex helps sleep come to him easily, it seems to have to opposite effect on me. I hate the nights, it's odd how the darkness and the quietude of night seem to enhance all human doubt. I look at his strong body asleep so peaceful next to me, the immensity of his the brute power cannot be denied. I snuggle into his warm body marveling at how even though a man and a woman are seemingly poles apart, appear to fit together side by side in their nakedness with perfection. Yes, the beauty of nature and the mystery of it.

I know at times I think too much, I probe too deep, but it is the essence of my being. I am no good at lying, yet lie I have. I wrestle with stopping my writings. These lifesaving incriminating documents, laying my feelings and fears into words, but I cannot.

THE BASEMENT

Sunday afternoon I could not find Cleo. Master had stepped out to the shops, I am beginning to believe that these walls will be my only world. He has not taken me from this house since my arrival, and I am starting to believe he never will. The thought scares me, but I hope in time he will see that if he takes me out I will be a very good girl, and he will no longer have any reason for me not to accompany him.

I called for Cleo but she did not come. I fretted perhaps she had slipped out of the door as Master left? She had become as curious as I about the world outside of late. I walked to the front door and I must confess until now I had never even considered trying to open it. I felt like a thief as I placed my hand on the worn brass door knob and turned it slowly, but the door was locked fast, as was the back door, and I could see Cleo nowhere outside.

I decided to resume my search of the basement, my cat often frequented there looking for mice. There was only a bare light bulb toward the front of this dreary, dank space, just enough light to do the washing by. The rear of the long narrow basement was in pitch darkness, it seemed to me no one had bothered to venture back here for a very long time. There was a small dividing stone wall that only ran partially across, dividing the space, the black bulk of the boiler stood directly behind it. There was a vast quantity of old stuff stored here, most of it now destroyed by the encroaching and pervasive mold. There was a small tunnel running through the stored and forgotten items and I ventured back there calling my kitten, wishing I had a torch. I looked up at the floor studs overhead, old soot and crumbling stone fell in my eyes, it hurt.

I reached the back of this fetid place in the darkness and my questing hand contacted with a cool vertical piece of steel. I had expected crumbling stone, not a barred door. I let my eyes adjust to the gloom and I realized what I was looking at was a tiny cell carved into the earth. It was only large enough to crouch in or stand. The door was well made and a recent addition, it certainly had not been part of the old original house. Again that sick feeling rose in me. Master had not made an idle threat about locking me up that day, and I turned to be gone. It was just as well, as I reached the washing machine I heard the front door slam, and I knew I had failed to be at the door naked and waiting as he liked.

Sheepishly I ascended the rough wooden stairs, took my clothes off and knelt at his feet amongst the bags of groceries on the floor. Cleo who had now miraculously appeared, investigating the new items. "Getting tardy are we slave?" I knew I was about to get hit for my transgression.

He administered the prescribed punishment with unerring precision in his usual fashion with the belt. Tied over his bed and gagged. All I could think was at least this time he was not hunting for a confession, and I was grateful for small mercies. He then let me up to do him the honor of cooking and serving him his dinner, and all the while I wondered had he ever really kept someone down there, confined in the dark?

OF BIRTHDAY'S

It's my mother's birthday today she will be forty-five, still young by today's standards, and yet I know better. I think of her and I know she is truly one of those who long ago lost her soul, she is a mere husk of the woman I am sure she once was. Not that I can speak with any authority for I only know her as she is today. Her life in so many ways a normal one, she chose a man and entwined her future with his. She bore him three children and followed his downward spiral across two continents. A mere chattel to a man who openly treated her with disdain, and beat her behind closed doors. Am I any different? I would like to think so, or am I just reliving my mother's life over in a more modern setting? Perhaps I am and I stand accused of repeating her mistake. However I do not see in Master the idle loser my father was, nor do I see the silent resignation of my mother in myself, but then I am only 18 and I wonder what I might be like at 25, let alone at 45 so far away as to be almost unimaginable.

It's Master's twenty-eighth birthday on Monday and he informed me he is going to celebrate it early on Saturday here at home with some friends and that I had better be on my best behavior. I did not like the menace in his tone, and the idea of his friends quite frankly made me nervous. Still I assured myself I should not be so cynical, just maybe they might be wonderful people and somewhat enjoyable company, and usually at a party there were many people, loud music and the doors would be left open. Perhaps once I met a few of his friends he may gradually relax his tight hold, and take me out a little?

I lamented the fact I had no money and could not furnish Master with a present myself. Just like I could not send my mother one, but I have never held a job nor had anything other then a little pocket money, so its hard to miss what one has never had. Though the regret was there.

That evening Master stood at the doorway, my hair trailing over his work boots as I knelt at his feet in my gesture of submissive greeting. It used to be a hard thing for me to bring myself to do, but now it comes to me so naturally. I could see he had been clothes shopping, and I ruefully wished he would take me along. "My friend helped me choose these for you." He said pointing at the bags. I wondered who he meant by friend? "I want you to look beautiful for me this Saturday when my friends kom." He was lapsing into Danish again, but at least I was beginning to understand what he said.

I was excited he had chosen to present me with some new things, and he watched me without a word as I examined what he had bought for me. There was a beautiful black dress, it was short and of the sheerest material, backless with a halter top. I loved the shoes, shining black patent leather, with four inch platforms and long spiked heels. I put them on immediately and they made me feel so tall. I was almost level with Master's eyes and I could tell he liked them on me too.

He smiled, his broad smile of approval showing his even white teeth. Then it occurred to me he had bought me no underwear and I fretted he would make me wear the belt under the dress, visible to all. It worried me so I could not let the matter lie. He laughed at my concern. "No, I want you to wear nothing under that." I was not sure whether to feel relieved or mortified.

That Saturday we slept very late, not rousing until well after twelve. I made sure the small house was as tidy and as ready for guests as possible. I could see Master had bought vast quantities of alcohol, he was really intending to have a very large party. He had also bought a good amount of food, to him it was party food, but to me it seemed all very ordinary. He wanted me to make many sandwiches with all kinds of breads and weird things in them, some of them I know would never pass my lips like the ones with the awful herrings in.

Still he was patient with me, trying to explain that is what they ate at a party, it did not seem very delicious to me. Many European foods did not. The cheeses so strong, and all the scary meats and fish, not to mention the rollmops. That done he told me to go get ready and to look my best.

Looking back at myself in the mirror I see Myra the simple slave girl, yet I do not. My hair up, the sophisticated dress, and the make up that makes me seem older, and with these props I can be someone else. I like the feeling, I feel braver, more confident, sexy. The feeling dissolves as I hear the first knock at the door, and it is replaced by fumbling uncertainty and fear. I linger in the safety of the bedroom as the first guests arrive, apparently quite forgotten. Master is talking loudly in a very animated fashion greeting his friends. I only catch a few words, nothing important or out of place. It appears he has not seen many of them for a long time and he is delighted to finally catch up.

I peeked hesitantly around the door, and I realized all of his guests were male. I also observed even though one likes to believe all white people are fairly similar you can see they are of his country. I am sure if I sighted an American among them I would have instinctively known. Some subtle thing makes people of each nation different. Master sighted me and I did all I could to look natural and relaxed as he beckoned me to his side and proceeded to introduce me to his guests. They seemed decent enough, some spoke in halting English, and some very well. It was embarrassing to be asked how I liked it here, and I found myself covering the fact I had been nowhere at all. I caught sight of Master once during the early part of the evening, he was watching me do this and relishing my discomfort.

His guests liked to drink and they had all brought more alcohol of their own to add to the already large stockpile. The house was filling up with all these strange people and the music was loud. I gravitated to the rear of the room to be where I felt most comfortable, and unobserved. Master was holding court with what I assumed were some of his closest friends. They were drinking copious amounts of schnapps, many of them smoking, most of them, young, strong and vital like Master was. I saw his brother walk in, his somber gray eyes alighting on me almost instantly. He smiled at me and nodded, I smiled nervously back. He was met by Master, the two men bear hugged one another in a display of their brotherly affection, then joined the group and I plucked at the hem of my dress conscious of my lack of underwear.

A man a lot shorter than the others entered the room, he was dressed in black well worn bike leathers. I knew where I had seen him instantly, in the awful photos with the sad girl. On seeing him Master looked for me immediately, and I knew instinctively these two men shared the same dark secrets. Master guided me over to him, my senses flooded with fear. I did not wish to be anywhere near him. He was probably somewhere in his early to mid thirties it was hard to say. He was not threatening in stature, he was not large, though I could see he was still powerful. It appeared he lived the good life, his waist had thickened and he had quite a belly. His oily hair was long and of the darkest brown, combed back, it's length to just below his shoulders, and it was thinning markedly in the front. He had a bushy goatee and the darkest eyes, the kind you cannot see the pupils in. I feared him, I truly did. He exuded badness and I wanted nothing to do with him.

"Mick this is Myra." Master introduced us. I could hear the lust thickening Master's voice, or was it just the alcohol? I squeaked the feeblest hello. Mick did not smile but just looked at me in a dead pan fashion from head to toe. I could see he had numerous scars on his face. He turned to Master grinning.

"Nice." Was all he said, and with that the men went back to the drinks and the food. The room smelled of smoke and fish, and I felt ill. The doors were both open even though it was far from warm, and I lingered by the back door trying to get some fresh air. Looking out at the yard and the sleeping tree waiting for summer, thinking it was just as well I had locked Cleo down in the basement. All this activity would have been frightening for her, it was bad enough for me.

I heard a loud exclamation from the front room and I crossed the kitchen floor to see what the source of the noise was. My eyes were greeted by the vision of a beautiful woman, and Master was at her side instantly inviting her to sit with him. The two of them kissed evoking feelings of desolation and betrayal in me I cannot describe. She was tall, very tall, in high heels she was taller than Master was, graceful and slender. Her dress was short, so very short, it was of black leather that hugged her athletic body. I could only describe her as an amazon. Her hair was long and red and was clasped in a long pony tail like thick rope, her cheekbones high and sculpted she exuded pride in her every movement. She proceeded to smoke a cigarette in a holder, Master did not waste any time lighting it for her. It disturbed me to see him do it. I felt crumpled and small as I observed her from the kitchen doorway. I had never seen a woman like her before, at least not in real life.

By this hour those who did not enjoy the drink and the growing lewd conversation, had begun to politely give Master their well wishes and depart. I could see Master was being left with a core of his more raucous friends who were intending to do some serious heavy drinking. The haughty woman amongst them showing no sign of leaving either. I picked at some fruit in the kitchen and decided to venture into the back yard. I stood at the step a long time it was dark and the narrow lane way behind Master's house quiet. The chill breeze made me shiver and I heard a stray cat in the dumpsters beyond the high fence that encircled the postage stamp of a yard. I walked out into the night the first time I had done so for one and a half months. It felt strange to not be enclosed in four confining walls. My shoes spiked into the soft lawn and it was hard to walk but I went to the centre of the yard and breathed the cool night air in, delighting in it, listening to the impersonal sounds of the city.

"What are you here doing?" I jumped, almost falling over as my heel sunk into the lawn, but it was not Master it was his brother. He had noticed my exodus when no one else had. I did not know what to say and made to swiftly return inside. He caught me as I made to pass him and held me to him. I did not look up, I did not want to encourage him in any way.

"You are so køn Myra." I knew he meant beautiful, Master said it to me numerous times it was one of the Danish words I had learned. I did not acknowledge him, still he held me fast, his large hand beginning to appraise me further in places I did not like. He was drunk but not so drunk he was out of control. I backed away. Still the alcohol had loosened his tongue and as he held me he attempted to tell me in his broken English how much he missed his wife. He was hard to understand, coupled with the fact I was trying to head off his unwanted advances. He pushed me into the corner of the kitchen cupboards and I found I had nowhere else to run, his hand up my dress.

Some of Master's friends came into the kitchen, but paid me little attention. I heard someone call me luder, I knew the word to mean whore, but no one seemed to care Master's brother was intending to use me on the bench top. I tried to push him off me but I could not, and in the next moment I had the canister of salt in my hand and flung it at his face. He roared in anger as the salt stung his eyes, but it was all I needed to slide from under him and escape. I ran to the other side of the room only to be confronted with a wall of men looking through the kitchen door to see source of the commotion, my Master standing foremost amongst them. The proud woman had not moved from her place nor did she seem at all interested in my plight.

Master looked at me, I withered under his stare. "You need to learn to relax and have a good time Myra." His words were slurred he was very drunk that was quite plain. "I can see I will have to help you." His friends laughed, and his brother glowered at me from the other end of the kitchen cheated of his conquest. Master took a small metal pill box out of his jeans pocket and flicked off the lid with his thumb. He poured some pills into his hand and closed it again returning it to his pocket. I could not believe nearly everyone here just stood watching, but that is exactly what they did. I felt like I was trapped in a den of wolves.

Master took his eyes off me for a moment and looked at his brother exchanging some wordless meaning. I felt deflated realizing no matter what I did they would always be on the same side, brothers in blood and ideals, and I their helpless puppet. Master came towards me skirting the small table where we ate breakfast, closing the back door as he did so. I felt like a wild horse being approached for the first time, and I struggled as I felt his brother's hands on my wrists. He took the handful of pills and forced me to swallow them massaging my throat to be sure they really went down. "Good girl." He said victoriously his breath heavy with spirits, his eyes sparkling. "Now you can kom and join in my party." He guided me between his guests back into the lounge room.

I will not lie I've tried a few substances in my short life time, most at Master's behest but never in this setting. I sat there beside him, the beautiful woman gazing at me disdainfully with her cool blue-gray eyes. I remember Master introducing me to her. Her name was Birgitte. I believe I was as about as significant to her as an ant.

Then as the pills began to work, things began to get indistinct and weird. I remembered moments, frozen snippets of the remainder of the evening. Disturbing and frightening images and I am not sure if I imagined them or not? I know Master used me in front of everyone on the coffee table and I think he gave me to Mick as well. I remember Mick holding me down, and at one point I was tied to the iron bed with Master telling me to hold still. I was trying to speak but my tongue would not form words. I recall vividly the woman looking at me and her cruel smile, it was hauntingly cruel.

INDELIBLE INK

It was well into the afternoon when I did wake. I felt sick and my head hurt. I fought down the pressing urge to vomit. My body was sore inside and out. I was not in Master's familiar arms but the heavily inked ones of his brother. Even though I was in Master's bed, he was nowhere to be seen.

They had tied me to it, it had not been a dream. The ropes were still there hanging from the bed frame, and it was then I spied the black ink of a tattoo on my lower belly. In disbelief I brushed it with my hand, the black inked edges were raised and angry, it was sore and weeping, and it was very real. The Letters F and E entwined, my Master's initials in beautifully executed black font. The words, a tattoo is forever rose in my mind, and before I could stop myself I began to cry unabashed tears of grief, rising to a loud wailing.

I found I could not stifle my outpouring of emotion. Master's brother stirred putting his arms about me, soothing me with his Danish words, and holding me to him, rocking me in the bed like I was a small child. No one else stirred in my distress and he just continued to tell me everything was all right until I could cry no more.

The day was a complete right off. Master surfaced late in the afternoon, he was sick as well, much sicker than I. I heard him at one point vomiting in the bathroom and I did not see him until the day was almost done. He stood in the bedroom doorway looking at me sitting in the bed, his brother slumbering oblivious beside me. I looked at him accusingly, and in that moment I felt hate.

"Kom." Was all he said in a sickly voice hoarse from excessive drinking. I wrapped myself in my favorite blanket, it was cobalt blue and hand crochet by my grandmother whom I had never met. It's one of my few and only possessions and very dear to me. He sat on his chair and bid me to stand in front of him. The room was strewn with bottles, dirty glasses, leftovers, and brimming stale ashtrays. I looked about taking in the aftermath, knowing I would be expected to dumbly tidy this all up without so much as a word.

He tugged the blanket from my shoulders, his eyes on my lower belly and the fresh ink work there. He put his fingers on the letters, it hurt, as he traced them I flinched. He did not falter, he seemed to be having some kind of spiritual experience at seeing his initials forever stamped on a living human body. He pulled me closer and in a gesture of great tenderness he kissed the marks. "You are mine Myra, forever mine." He whispered, in a voice laden with desire. Again I felt overcome with tears. I collapsed to my knees before him and sobbed with wild abandon wetting the carpet at his feet.

Through my tears I was suddenly aware Master was talking to me, and I fought them aside so I might concentrate on his voice. He stopped talking patiently waiting for me gather my emotions under control. I looked up into his face framed in his thick golden hair, his usually clear eyes were bloodshot. In the darkening room he looked like some hellish denizen. I stiffened and for the second time that day I felt anger and even hatred toward him, and all of his kind. I wanted to slap his arrogant face, drag my nails through his eyes, anything to make him hurt as he had hurt me. The feeling ran so deep I was ill prepared for the force of it, the blackness in my soul. Instead all I said to him was. "Why?"

He sat for some moments taking me in before he replied in a lazy voice. "Since time began Myra this is what it is, and always has been. Man is the Master and woman is his slave. It's only the little niceties of the society we inhabit today that allow a few women to think and feel otherwise, but any day they can fall, any day they could become just as you, a slave, and once a slave, always a slave." His voice was low almost a growling whisper, and he leant down toward me his long hair tickling my skin.

"It's the tattoo that bothers you isn't it Myra?" I nodded in affirmation. I know he had spoken about marking me but I had never really thought he was serious, and all I could think of was the sad woman with the black sun in the same place I wore his initials. I was not thinking right or clearly and he knew it. He was hoping to capitalize on the aftermath of my disoriented state, but he did not need to, my lips had already betrayed me.

"The girl with the sun here." I pointed to his mark. "Was she yours too?" Master paused, I could see he was thinking carefully. Even with a hangover he had a mind like a steel trap. So I was surprised at his answer, I had expected vehement denial.

"Once......." He said wistfully, like he was remembering some far distant time. "You have been looking at my photos haven't you? Of Gabrielle?" His green orbs bored into me and I nodded yes under his scrutiny. "I see." He said and sighed. "No Myra you are not the first and you will probably not be the last." I felt chilled at his casual admission, and it appeared to him to be no big deal. Had I not offered my all to him? "It was a long time ago before I met you." He elaborated. "I was twenty then. I picked her up in Amsterdam. She was a run away and a drug addict, and I made her my slave. It was easy, all too easy. There are lots of girls like her."

"What happened to her?" I felt compelled to ask. He smiled down at me, a wry grin on his stubbled face.

"She was not like you Myra." Was this his feeble attempt at assurance? I could not tell. He went on and I let him talk. It was rare he spoke like this and even rarer to hear him explain himself. "She was just there, she filled a need." My mind flashed back to the distressing pictures of torture and mutilation all too alive on the computer screen. "I did not love her like you, she was there, but you Myra you are beautiful. Beautiful in your innocence, and your dependance in a way she could never be." He seemed frustrated as he tried to express this, almost as though he was about to get angry. I did not press him further my own anger had long ago subsided. Behind him I heard his brother stirring in the bedroom, the light flicked on casting streams of bright light across the floor. Master was still not finished with his explanation. "She got too much for me. I could not trust her to be good." I really wondered what he meant by that and I thought of the small cell in the basement, and I shuddered. "I gave her to Mick, he is a good friend of mine, I knew he could give her what she needed. He took care of her for a while but she had an overdose and died............. And now I have you." He poked his big finger at my chest. "And you Myra, are not going anywhere."

I did finally pluck up the courage last night to ask Master if the beautiful woman Birgitte was the friend he was referring to when he spoke of being helped to choose my clothes. He seemed to have no problem telling me yes she was, and he also added she was very helpful in procuring for him many things, including my anti baby pills as he so quaintly put it. I could not believe that his network of help in my enslavement could be so thorough. He had obviously thought about all this a long time, and planned it very carefully.

HE WHO CAN TAKE ANYTHING AWAY

Master does not do much with me week nights, he is tired after his long days of menial heavy work, and plants himself in his chair, his intense eyes half closed gazing at the television in the dark room. He sits silent most evenings with only the subtlest of gestures to indicate his glass needs filling, or for some other need. I serve him in silence, wrapped in my blanket by his feet, leaning against the front of his chair ready to jump at his slightest inclination. I try hard for him, there are times I feel I try so hard my heart will burst, and I can try no more.

Sometimes he just bewilders me completely. However weekends are an entirely different matter, it seems he always has something in store. I have learned on Friday's to be ready for his visitations into excess, and this Friday I kneel and wait even before I hear his keys in the door lock. He has told me not to bother with dinner and I wonder what that means for me? Perhaps we are having takeaway?

He often pays me no heed. I'm sure he looks at me but he does not acknowledge my presence at all and goes to the pile of the mail on the desk. Tossing the junk mail on the floor. Cleo often purrs around me in tight circles tickling my naked flesh. I have noticed she does not do this to Master and seeks to avoid him, she will not even seek his lap when he is in his chair. Perhaps animals are wiser than we humans are?

He will often make me wait a long time before he desires me to move from my position. I am sure it pleases him to see me there in some oblique fashion, but I feel very confused why such an attractive man as he is, needs this to fuel his ego? I sense tonight will not be routine, he leaves me to wait. I can feel a slight cold draught coming under the door, and wish summer would come.

"Myra." I hear him call me from the kitchen. I still jump when he talks to me in that tone, and my heart is already racing. I cross the threadbare carpet. I see he has pulled the kitchen table to one side and has placed the chrome chair in the centre of the room. "Sidde!" He commands and taps the chair. I do as he says, the chromed steel cold on my skin. He leaves the room I can hear him in the bedroom it sounds like he is tearing the place apart. I should be scared, and well I am, but all I can think of is the mess he is making.

He returns with some lengths of rope and a rubber mask. I don't like the look of it, it is heavy, and I have never seen it before. Master is not one for toys he is a spontaneous man, generally using what is as hand. I sit meekly and let him fasten me to the chair, and while he does it I listen to his breathing and the distant sounds of the city outside and contemplate why I let him do this? I already know why, but knowing does not make it any easier to understand. The chair is already slick from my excitement, but the major reason is even if I said no he would just enforce his will. He ties me well. I cannot move and he stands before me. I look at his stomach, it's flat and hard, his whole body is hard like flesh made into steel. So very different from mine. He is all I am not.

"I want to show you something Myra?" I'm afraid of what is coming. I nod but other than that I cannot move in the tight bindings. Disturbingly I discover I need to pee, and I wish I had had the foresight to have gone before he had come home. The need is there but for the time being I can push it aside. "I want you to truly realize I can take anything away from you my slave." A smile twists the corner of his mouth just enough to catch a glimpse of his teeth, perhaps more a grimace than a smile. His eyes are cold. I tremble at what he is alluding to? He pulls my long straight hair back, brushing my face with his rough hands, making sure it is well out of the way. He picks up the mask and pulls it over my head. Its tight, so very tight and has no eye holes. My hair is pulling, further adding to my discomfort. I strain to hear what he is doing.

"Like your eyes Myra, I can take your sight from you, any time I want." I sit, whispering the tiniest yes. He then grabs me under the chin and pushes his fingers into the sides of my face forcing me to open my mouth. He knows just where to push. I fight him with this every time, I'm fearful of being gagged I feel as though I will suffocate, especially if I cry and my nose gets all blocked, and I know I am going to cry. He pushes the object into my mouth, and I am horrified to realize it is an inflatable gag. It fills my mouth totally, and I find myself wondering where it has been, but germs are the least of my problems. Already I am panicking for breath, I do all in my power to try to calm down. I cannot afford to cry or panic, or I will lose my ability to breathe clearly through my nose.

"I can take your speech as well." I hear him say, as he again leaves for the bedroom. My heart is pummeling in my chest. I try ever so hard to attempt to control my need to breathe more air than my nose will allow, while I strain to hear what he is up to. I find myself rhythmically sucking on the gag trying to gain control like some primal reflex left over from when I was an infant.

He returns in a short space of time. I am becoming exceedingly uncomfortable, but I can tell he does not care. He is standing behind me, he pulls my head back and begins to fit what I believe is another mask over the one I already have on. It is even heavier than the first, and I feel most distressed when he buckles it tightly about my throat. The position of my steel collar making it feel even worse, and its now becoming hard to hear.

"This is the fun part Myra." Even through my muffled hearing I can hear his unbridled glee. He does not elaborate but stands quietly behind me for some time, and it creeps into my conscience slowly I am running out of air. At that moment even though I am tied I can feel the lightheadedness coming on, I thrash in my bonds. Pure panic drives me as I realize he is going to stand there and let me suffocate.

Finally the sweet gift of air, in the smallest measured dose. I have not felt such pure primal panic ever. I wanted to be able to speak, I needed to tell him to stop. I tried to through the gag but it was impossible. "Shush." Was all he said, and I knew he was on the precipice of his own release as he was standing behind me watching me thrash about. He hung over the back of the chair when he was done, close to my ear, I could feel his long hair brushing my shoulders, and his warm semen dripping down the small of my back.

"I can take anything away Myra, anything." He rasped. His words chilled me and I knew he was right. I just nodded and hoped he was satisfied and would not do it again. To my relief he removed the breath control mask and the gag. My mouth was sore and tasted of rubber, but before I could shut it he was forcing his partially flaccid cock in to it. I took the length of it tasting the remnants of his semen, he just stood very still. I felt the hot stream as he began to piss in my mouth, slowly at first. Urine was so bitter. I hated having to do this, but I swallowed dutifully. "Good girl." He cooed, patting my head and holding me so I could not pull away.

He left me then, and I heard him taking a shower. The sound of the running water rekindling my urgency to relieve myself. He lingered long in the bathroom and I wished I was in there with him, massaging his broad back as he liked me to do, and enjoying the hot water as it washed away the dirt and cares of his day. A day I could only imagine at. His life in many ways is mythology to me. To my aggravation he did not even pay me a second glance but instead sat in his chair. The television went on in the dark room beyond and I sat miserably trying to fight my growing bodily demands.

Being blinded I do not know how long I sat but eventually I could take no more. I was shivering, this only increased my screaming desire to urinate, and worse I could not feel my hands or feet. I was trying to move them wriggling my toes and fingers. I finally broke down and called for him. He did at least come into the kitchen immediately. "What do you want Myra?" The question was absurd, he knew what I wanted but he made me beg him anyway.

"I need to get up......please." I offered. My distress quite plain. Still he stood making no move to free me.

"What you need and what you get Myra are two different things, don't you think?" He opened the fridge and I could hear him pouring a drink. I did not wish to play this game of his it had gone on for long enough already.

He came back to stand before me and I jumped as I felt his fingers massaging my clit. He knew just where to touch he was very adept at this. "No........" I said, and even as I said it I choked it down, the one word he had told me he never wanted to hear from my lips. I waited for him to hit me or retaliate in some way but he did not. He just kept the pressure on my clit, and I could feel my bladder relaxing as he did it.

"What is it Myra?" He said persuasively. "Your body is your enemy, not I. It betrays you." That was it then, he wanted me to beg, so beg I did. Unabashed, unashamed begging to be released. "No Myra." Was all he said. Never had I felt more miserable or powerless, and he kept up his assault on my physical control until I pissed myself.

I think in that moment he chipped a piece of my humanity away, he had made me feel like a trapped animal harnessing my primal need to reduce me to total weakness and despair. His method, my madness. His point made he released me from the chair, calling me. "Dumme kælling." A dumb bitch, and I spent the remainder of the miserable evening cleaning up the linoleum in the kitchen.

THE LETTER

The mail fell through the door with a loud thud on the carpet. I should know this by now, yet every day if I am not paying attention it still sends my heart racing. I have even been known to drop items, or spill my drink. Silly really, have I become so timid, or was I always this way?

Every day I pick up the mail and take a cursory look at it. Mostly it is to me of little personal interest, dull white envelopes I am sure contain nothing but bills. They look the same the world over.

Sometimes I look through the advertisements and wonder if I will ever have the simple pleasure to walk hand in hand with Master through a shopping mall, eating ice cream, maybe seeing a movie, or looking at nice clothes? I think I know the answer but I refuse to believe it. My eyes fill with tears blurring my ability to further read, and dampening my desire to dream. I place all the items on the computer desk and stare ruefully out of the window wondering where are all the beautiful things? I turn on the swivel chair and look a the eclectic contents of Master's home. Perhaps men do not need or care for them to inhabit their world?

Cleo lands in my lap to ease my sadness, she has an unerring ability to sense when I need comfort. As I hold her and peer into her questioning green gold eyes I find beautiful things are still in sight. I chide myself for not seeing them before. I must not lose sight of the beauty there is even here in my tiny prison in a foreign land.

Today is different, there is a brightly colored envelope among the drab letters that grace the floor. It is from America and addressed to me. I pick it up, I know the handwriting anywhere, it's my mothers. I want to tear it open immediately such is my excitement. My nails begin to tear at the top corner of the envelope but I stop. I am torn, in a debate with my conscience and his edicts. Will he allow me to open this without him present? I so desire to and I wrestle with myself long moments finding I cannot tear the envelope from the letter. Part of me cannot believe I am indeed wrestling with this, after all it is my letter. I find I cannot open it, and instead I place it on top of the pile to await his return that I may read it as he glances over my shoulder, wanting to digest all it's contents however insignificant they seem.

I sat staring at the blank piece of paper the pen gripped in my hand. I had so much to say yet none of it could I commit to paper. I wanted so badly to reach out to my mother and tell her at last I understood. Tell her what a hero I thought she was. However all that I did finally manage to pen there were simple niceties and white lies. "Of course I am loving it here." He's been so fabulous to me." "His family are wonderful." Master read every word, watched me put it in the envelope, seal it. He took it from me on his way to work, I assume he posted it. If he approved of the content that is.

DEEP INSIDE

Saturday afternoon we were 'graced' with the presence of Mick. Master insisted I answer the door for him naked and kneel before him. Master is trying very hard to get me used to the idea of pleasing other men but this particular man I find I am greatly repulsed by, and I think Master is well aware of it. I cringe under his dark scrutiny, and I am still not sure Master did not let him have me at his party. He assures me he did not, but I do not believe him. At the very least I know he was the artist of the hated tattoo that now adorns my body, and I find myself hating him all the more.

The two men sit, Master in his great chair and Mick his scuffed boots up on the lounge. They do not make any pretense at English. I bring them drinks and place them on the coffee table. I know enough to understand most of what they speak of is filthy. This man seems to bring out all that is the worst in Master, and I find myself so wishing he would no longer visit.

In a first Master offers me a drink from his own glass. I halt and I am unsure whether to take the proffered beverage or not. I attempt to make a polite refusal. He looks at me and insists I do so. I do as he wishes and he makes me drain the entire glass, it seems it is an expected custom here when drinking. The firewater he likes to drink is clear and strong, and I have difficulty getting it down. No sooner than I had managed to feel remotely normal again he was already finishing his and pouring me yet another, and I felt nothing but dread. I knew he had plans for me. The two men just sat and talked. Mick smoked one cigarette after the next rapidly filling the ashtray, I was glad Master did not smoke at all. I find it a repulsive habit. I lost count of the drinks I had consumed, and was feeling very lightheaded. I noted my ability to interpret anything they said had completely faded, their conversation nothing more to me than a drone in the background.

The alcohol had relaxed me and I was in no state to refuse when Master picked me up as though I was no more than a little girl and carried me to the bedroom. He sat me on the chair and I saw him strip off the quilt and lay towels on the bed. I tried to get up but he was already holding me, and effortlessly lifted me on to the bed. When I saw Mick framed in the doorway I began to resist and scream. Mick did not cross the threshold into the room, he just leant in the door opening and watched. Master shoved his hand over my mouth and held me down until I decided to stop. Drunk as I was it was not much of a fight and in the far recesses of my mind all I could think of was that girl. Were they like this with her?

"Quiet or I will put the hood on you again? Master threatened. The memory still very fresh in my mind commanded me to sudden silence. "That's better." He said. "Much better." Taking the rope and fastening me spread-eagled to the bed I felt hot with shame, or was it just the effect of the drink? Mick came into the room and settled into the chair his furry chin resting on his hands. I could see his many large silver rings.

"Don't hurt me?" I pleaded to Master as he tied my hands to the top of the bed frame. He just stroked the side of my face and smiled.

My head swam and I fought to clear my wits, the alcoholic haze would not shift. Master forced another glass of it between my lips and I decided it would be easier to just lie there and let them get on with it, whatever might come. I closed my eyes, it beat looking at a wavering ceiling. The lube felt ice cold as Master pushed it inside of me. Why he needed so much of it was beyond me but I was by now in a place beyond caring. They were talking but I could not understand any of it, their laughter unnerved me.

I felt Master's fingers slide into me, first one, then two, the tightness mounting as he kept adding another finger. The drink had done its work and I was very relaxed. What he was getting out of this I did not know but it did not feel all too bad. Though where he had cut me long ago was beginning to hurt, and I began to go into myself, to the place that I found could sometimes help me manage the pain and the panic. Master's hands are very large, by the time he had all four fingers in me even in my inebriated state I could feel it. I felt more than a little uncomfortable with the pressure he was exerting.

When he withdrew his fingers it was a relief until I registered Mick was taking up where he had left off. I made a futile gesture to evade him with my very limited capacity to move. Master was now sitting on the bed beside me gently stroking my hair and urging me to be still. I gave up and began to cry. I could feel

Mick's hand slide right into me, and I saw the evil gleam of satisfaction on his face, Master seemed unmoved. The pressure inside was hard to describe, the ultimate form of possession. I could see why Master had chosen to get me half drunk, and I felt grateful he had shown me this mercy. I kissed his hand and he smiled at me and told me I was a very good girl. Words I rarely hear, and words that have the capacity to make me melt.

The towel beneath me was soaked. Master kissed me one last time his lips lingering gently on my forehead. Mick had retreated to the chair my insides feeling strangely open and empty. Though not for long, it seemed Mick's violation was only in preparation for Master's final assault. His four fingers now slid in more easily than before. I groaned as he pushed further and fought my rising panic as my insides really began to hurt. I was so afraid I would tear, his knuckles passing my body's final resistance. I bucked on the bed pulling against the ropes that held me fast as he pushed his entire hand inside. I felt so full like he might tear my insides from me. It was a supremely erotic sensation once I could get past the pain, coupled with raw fear. He could sense it, his predatory green eyes locked on mine and for the first time, nothing existed but he and I, no surrounding walls, no Mick, there was nothing in the world, just us. The words he so loved me to say ushered from my mouth. The secret ones I often spoke to him in the dark, the powerful words that could make him cum. "I am your slave. Yours to use. Yours to punish. Yours to love." At last I began to understand the intensity and unwavering trust between Master and slave.

I felt tender and sore all of Sunday, Master seemed very pleased with me after Saturday afternoon. He was most loving and even thoughtful. He had pushed me beyond one of my biggest fears and he knew it. My fear not some childhood one fueled by naive ignorance, but one created by Master himself. Perhaps he felt he was rehabilitating me? Undoing his wrong? Ever since Master cut me I feel intense panic and fear when anything foreign enters me. Even things designed for the purpose. I believe a man at least can feel what he is doing and he can sense if it is wrong, but a foreign object cannot. I can see why Master chose to ply me with drink, and I have decided I must trust him more, perhaps indeed he does know what is best. I feel changed by yesterday's experience.

OUR BABY

It was late Tuesday evening. We had finished dinner which Master most often chose to eat in the lounge room as he halfheartedly watched a movie or the news. He would never settle on a channel and it seemed if I became engrossed in anything in particular he would just as swiftly, with no regard for me, change the channel breaking my interest. I had taken to not really watching the television at all because of the futility of it, and I could not understand the majority of it anyway. Most week nights it was just us, and this evening was no exception. I looked across at the computer sitting innocently on the desk, Master's e-mail open on the screen and contemplated my guilt at attempting to communicate to the world.

"I want to talk to you." Master's words pulled me out of my self examination. He indicated I sit at his feet, and I hurriedly ran over the events of the day fretful I had erred in some duty that he may have found disappointment in. He put his hand on his stubbled chin in a gesture of great thought, absently rubbing his jaw. "I have been thinking Myra. About the future and us." All I could hope was that this was a good thing, perhaps finally a ray of light in my bleak existence was coming to pass? ".......And I have decided that we should have a child."

I did not fail to notice he had said, I. He smiled down at me like this news of his would make me the happiest woman in the world. If he expected me to respond in feverish joy he did not get his wish. I felt like I had been hit by a car. I did not know how to respond, and I could not believe his sudden change of heart. He had always told me unwaveringly he never wanted any children. Not now, not ever.

"This will be a good thing." He continued. "You will have something to focus on here while I work." I struggled with his reasoning, this was a child, not some sudden flight of fancy, something you could give up on, or give away if it didn't work out. I could hardly see us raising one the way Master chose to live. I was only eighteen, and he ten years older than I but it seemed at this moment I was the adult here.

I was not sure if he wanted my opinion or not, but this was too serious to let lie. I had to speak my peace. I told him I was not ready, that I was way too young, that we were not married, and I was not legal here. I knew by the look in his eyes I was treading dangerous ground. He grasped my shoulders firmly and looked me in the eye. "I feed you, I put the clothes on your back, you sleep in my bed and under my roof, and you are telling me my child is not good enough for you?" I did not know how to answer. No matter what I said he would condemn me. So I said nothing. "Tell Me Myra." He growled menacingly. I could see his anger rising rapidly to the fore. "Does the fact I wish to let you have my child not honor you?" It was a loaded question, if I answered no he would beat me for sure, if I answered yes he would assume I sanctioned the idea.

"That's not what I was saying." I tried to counter, feeling like a trapped animal. "Of course it would be an honor, but I just don't think we are ready, so soon."

He sat, still holding me, his hands like talons gripping me tightly, he did not say anything for some time. I hoped fervently he was seriously considering what I had said. He sighed and shook his wild golden mane from side to side. "No Myra you just don't get it do you?" His voice barely more than a caressing whisper. He poked his finger hard at my breastbone. " You are my slave, my property. I decide what is best for you. And you my slave....... OBEY!"

This last word was shouted with full force at my face spraying me with his saliva. I winced and he thrust me to the floor. He stood up and towered over me. I was sure he was going to beat me. I unashamedly cowered pressing against the coffee table. He laughed one of his cruel laughs, and poked the hard toe of his steel cap boot into my ribs, with just enough force to make it hurt, but not enough to cause damage.

"You will have my child. I have decided and we will begin on it today." With that he wrenched me off the floor and dragged me to the bedroom.

True to his word Master took all my birth control pills and flushed them down the toilet, every single last one. He made me watch feeding on my obvious distress, and with that act I lost the last thing that separated me from women of ancient times, the ability to have any form of control over my body's fertility. I was damned with that act.

I have spent the last few days away from the computer completely. In some ways not visiting it made me feel calmer, sneaking behind Master's back is a terribly stressful endeavor. Yet I return, because I feel the need to converse with others to make sense of my wild feelings. My thoughts have been far from idle, even in my daily deeds I find I am not, simple as they are. I have had much to dwell on for sure. Sometimes it is best to sit alone and clear one's mind to truly analyze my real inner feelings. I guess I can understand Master's desire, he is older than I. I just never really took the time to imagine him with a family. I guess again as with his promise of his mark on my flesh, I heard him but did not interpret his reality. My mistake.

A very large part of me wants his child, even as a little girl I would find myself daydreaming of a baby. My own family so fractured, I feel the need to make it right. If not in my childhood, then in the childhood of my own children. I am resigned, if the great mysterious powers that be wish it to happen, it will. Who am I to fight it, nor him. He is right, to carry his child will honor him. With that status possibly I can hope for a little more as his slave as well. Hope, yes thats all a slave has really, and I will hold on to it with all my heart.

As of late there has been little to report here in this my forbidden journal, life has settled down somewhat, but Master being the volatile creature that he is I know this he has the capacity to change at any moment. Yet I am grateful for this peaceful time. My mind is far from a place of peace and tranquility, however. I wait fervently for any sign my body has, or has not, conceived a child. I feel the same as I always have I cannot detect anything is different. I am most sure I would feel it if it was happening to me. I longed to be able to have the wisdom of my mother at this moment of screaming uncertainty.

I think most women long for a baby, if not early in their life at some point it becomes a focus. It is in our natures to give, and to love. At least it is in mine. I must confess I have spent a great deal of time thinking about it in recent days. Daydreaming what it would be like to create life and love a little one, our little one. Would he be different then? Would it be a little girl so like me, shy and demure, or a little boy golden and strong like he is. He would melt if I gave him a son I am sure. Even here unhappy things creep in to taint my beautiful pictures, cruel and dark possibilities. So dark I do not wish to voice them lest I make them real.

Today as I do on many afternoons after my chores are complete, I sit before this monitor, my window on the world. I answer my letters, chat with a few dear friends and enjoy my short time socializing before Master's dinner must be prepared, and his return.

I do not wish to justify my existence here as his slave, nor do I feel I need to quantify my reasons for what I have become. I am merely that which I am, no more, no less. I do understand that which I do is an act of rarity in it's self. Possibly insanity as well. Many have told me my slavery is that of the kind of bygone days. I think on this, is slavery really something of the past, or is it something we just pretend no longer exists? Many women who marry are they not doing just the same as I? One may disagree, but what about women in the third world? It is a hard fact they are seen as no more than chattel to their men. Only one percent of the world's wealth is owned by women and in places in the Middle East a woman's birth is not even recorded I believe. I am still of the mind it is, and truly will always be a man's world.

THE ACCIDENT

Today I make an unusually late entry. I do this for the most part to calm my sense of worry. It is strange how one can sense something is very wrong even when there appears no evidence to the contrary. Master had left for work as he did every morning. I cleaned the house, played with Cleo, and looked at the forbidden internet. Six p.m. came and went, as did seven p.m. Master sometimes does return late, he is not one to tell me of his plans. As the hours pass I sense today is different. I linger by the front window waiting for his car, but still no sign.

I have started to imagine frightening scenarios, what if he never did return? What would I do? Where would I go? As the time edged on to ten p.m., I am feeling decidedly fearful. I sit in the darkness staring into the street, Cleo purring, taking full advantage of my lap and my petting hands. She helps ease my mounting state of panic. I am glad of her company.

It was almost eleven before I saw the car stop in front of the house. It was not Master's car though. My heart raced as I saw a figure get out and walk purposefully towards the door, I knew even in the half dark it was Master's brother. He turned the key in the lock. I was unsure how I should react. With my blanket pulled about me I knelt on the floor as he entered the darkened house. He almost trod on me, his boots hurt as they collided with my outstretched fingers.

"Get up girl." Was all he said. I could hear the strain in his voice and cold tendrils of fear gripped me as I sensed something was very wrong. I had long ago learned not to speak out of place and waited for him to tell me his news. Which I sensed was going to be bad. He directed me into the kitchen and sat me in a chair, he followed suit. "My bro......... Your Master." He corrected. "Has had an accident." My world darkened on hearing those words and I was fearful to hear the rest of his announcement. "His leg got crushed at work, some steel fell on him. He's okay, but his leg is badly broken. He is at the hospital they are operating on him now. He was very insistent I come here and stay with you. So I will be here until he can come home."

My head reeled, I could not believe what I was hearing, and I was wondering what this meant for me? I had to assure myself everything would be all right. "He was very lucky." His brother continued. "But he will be in the hospital for a few days." I myself could hardly call having a broken leg lucky. I wanted to be there by his side, it was my place, and my duty.

"Can we go see him?" I ventured.

Master's brother just shook his head. "I think it is best if you stay here, he will be home soon, and you can look after him then."

I saw him looking at the coffee maker, I got up from the table to answer his non verbal request. He smiled at me fitting his fingers together and cracking his joints as he stretched lazily. "You would make a good wife." He said, and I knew he meant it. I could have kept my cool if he had not held up the key to my chastity belt. I could not believe Master had given it to him.

I made him coffee, he liked it black and strong with spoonfuls sugar, just like Master did. He spent some time winding down after dealing with his brother's emergency and did not make a move for bed until it was well after twelve. "Kom." He requested.

He was not my Master, and I side stepped his request telling him I would be right along after I cleared the dishes in the kitchen. There were not many, but I hoped that by the time they were done he would already be asleep and I could avoid him completely. I turned from him to the sink and did not expect the touch of a hand on my shoulder. "Kom." He repeated more insistently. He was like Master in many ways, but unlike Master his elder brother was a pool of calm, and I found dealing with him was like trying to push aside a solid stone wall.

Again he was not my Master, and I shrugged his hand from my shoulder. I had refused him before and I intended to again, and now without the ability to avoid a possible pregnancy it was paramount I did. I was sure that would have been what Master had wanted also. He did not leave but stood behind me. Neither commanding me to fulfill his wishes or backing down on his request. He was a very resolute man and I found his passive force most intimidating.

"You don't you like me do you Myra?" I could feel his warm bulk behind me. I had not expected him to come out with that, he almost sounded hurt. I did not know how to answer as I fumbled with the coffee cups in the sink enjoying the hot water on my hands. I hedged, hoping to pacify him.

"No, it's not that, you are a wonderful man. It's not that at all." I was repeating myself. "I know you are lonely, I know it must be hard." I tried to commiserate, obviously the recent loss of his wife had been very difficult for him. Not something one would expect at only thirty-eight.

"Yes, it is." He said pressing himself into my back. "Very hard."

I could have killed myself over my choice of words. He pulled me from the sink. I slapped at him and missed, he laughed catching his fingers in my collar. "I can see why Frej bought this, very useful." He commenced to drag me by it across the kitchen floor. I slid on the black and white linoleum catching my little toe painfully on an upraised join, my blanket fell to the floor. As he pulled me through the rooms I scanned wildly about for anything I might reach to hurt him with, but there was nothing. As he wrestled me through the bedroom doorway in desperation I bit his hand, it was no play bite I bit down as hard as I could. He snatched his bloodied hand away and yelled. "Lede sæk!" I knew it meant fucking bitch, he was now no longer his usual calm self. I almost fell backward but righted myself and ran back to the kitchen to sight his wallet and keys on the table top. The key! It was my freedom and I snatched it up, wrestling the appropriate one from the jumble of other unidentified keys. He was fast behind me, I had it in the lock and turned it. The door opened and there it was my passageway to sweet freedom.

I never even made the centre of the yard, I screamed loudly for help, it was late, the city sounds at their minimum I am sure many heard it. He was on me his hand planted over my mouth, wasting no time dragging me back inside. I tried to bite him again this time without success. He got me inside and slapped me hard, it stung immensely and cut the inside of my mouth.

"Hold kæft!" He shouted commanding me to shut up, forgetting I did not understand his language in his passion. He bolted the door and shoved the keys in his pocket. In some ways he was more fearsome than Master. Seeing this usually very placid man so enraged, I wondered in that fleeting moment if perhaps I had really screwed up. I had now possibly angered and alienated the only other person I may have been able to use to my advantage. I did not have long to debate this course, however. This time he hauled me to the bedroom, tied my hands together behind my back, and used me roughly, oblivious to my pain while I cried.

I did not sleep at all well, he seemed to. All night he snored close to my ear and I stared at the ceiling, wondering if Master would be, as his brother is in ten years time? Morning finally dawned and he stirred freeing me. I guess he had to go to work, I did not ask. I was just glad to have him gone. I made him breakfast, he gathered up his things. I was very happy he had overlooked something Master never did, the chastity belt, and I was congratulating myself on the wonderful day I was about to have.

I was very wrong. He grabbed me with suddenness this time catching me completely off guard, he did not mess about as he had in the past. He held me very firmly and pushed a gag into my mouth, and I was mortified to realize he was taking me to the basement. Down the stairs past the washing machine, the boiler and down the back into the dark. I tied to scream to no avail all I did was drool, I fought him for all I was worth. He said nothing and manhandled me into the dank space with unerring efficiency. I kicked at him and he slapped me, the marks from his hands raising hot welts on my skin. Why was I not surprised he possessed the key to this prison of my dread also? He padlocked each of my hands to the steel uprights of the door, and closed it. I would be forced to stand in this position until he returned.

"I cannot trust you after last night, so until my brother gets home it will be this. I have to go for work." He clicked off the light and left. When I heard the front door close, I began to fight the steel restraints and the gag with all I had. A gesture of futility on my behalf which only left me tired, sweating, and chilled.

For three days until Master returned from the hospital I have had to endure this daily imprisonment, in spite of my pleas he did not relent. I guess my near escape last Thursday evening scared him, and I kicked myself for being my own worst enemy. I've shivered here totally chilled, my legs finding it difficult to be forced to stand for such long hours cramp. I've ached with thirst, felt hungry, and worse pissed myself. I guess this is how those without hope spent their days locked up in dark mediaeval prisons. Three days was more than enough for me.

Each night my jailer would return in Master's absence, he would watch me like I was a high security detainee, make me shower and in spite of my discomfort which he seemed oblivious to, sit while I made him dinner. Then he would watch the television a while until he was ready for bed, where he would use me without reservation. He has taken to chaining my collar to the bed frame, making nights difficult as I often wake and have to ask him if I may pee. Officially I now feel too afraid to not comply with anything he wants.

HIS RETURN

I felt totally degraded as I emerged from the dark basement. I could not even look at him. Master sat enthroned in his great leather chair, his right leg in a cast, propped up on the ottoman and some pillows. His brother hovered behind me. I felt like I was entreating some all powerful monarch for his mercy. I knelt before him. I could smell the scent of the hospital on him alien in this setting, and realized I was getting used to my nakedness, it had become second nature, even proper. I wondered briefly if it was possible if I could forget I needed clothing all together and actually go about in public? The thought frightened me, is this how madness begins?

"I hear from my brother you have been very bad Myra." At least he used my name, I could cling on to some vestige of humanity. His voice stern and tired had my full attention. I nodded unable to bring myself to say a word. "Hum." He said thoughtfully. "I did not need you to make this worse, it was bad enough for me already. I was most worried about you Myra." Cleverly turning the conversation about as he often did to make it seem he was the one in most distress, when all knew otherwise. "So tell me why did you misbehave?"

Silence was my friend, it was my mantra, my comfort. Intuition had already told me that Master already knew all. This time I elected to appeal to his sense of pity. A possibly unrealistic hope as I knew that portion of him was very small. "I did not mean to go out side I really didn't!" I wailed.

"But you did!" He countered leaning forward, I could tell it hurt him to do so. I was already half hysterical. I had broken one of his major edicts, and I knew he was irritable and hurting, and would have little sympathy for my reasons. Still I pressed on and he sat and listened.

"The reason I did it Sir was for our baby. I did not want to risk having a baby you did not know was yours! I did it for you!" As I said this I grasped his lower calf earnestly. I fervently meant what I had said. He was silent a long time.

"I see." Was all he had to say, he seemed displeased. With is brother, or with me? He coughed and I felt him wince, his leg was obviously hurting him. He shifted a little awkwardly in his chair, the leather creaked under his weight.

"Well, lets hope nothing happens then shall we?" I had no idea what his statement portended, but it fills me with anxiety.

CARING FOR MASTER

It has been a trying and difficult week living with an obstinate and difficult man. I post this while Master is at his appointment, it is the only brief time I now get alone.

Master refused to use a wheelchair, though he was told he had to at all costs keep off his leg and stay immobile if he wanted it to heal properly. He paid the medic's warnings and advice little heed. Instead hobbling about on crutches, not easy in this small confined home. If I was ever his slave I feel the full burden of it now and have a whole new appreciation for anyone who looks after someone long term. They are true heroes. I keep telling myself daily it is only for a few weeks, and hopefully life will return to normal. He expects me to provide his every need.

He cannot lie down in the bed at night but now rules my world from his chair in the lounge room. Even to the point of insisting I sleep on the floor beside him. I know it is important to keep him busy and even though it is difficult he must move about periodically. He seems loathe to do this and I cannot force him. He is cold one minute and hot the next, and at times he is in a great deal of pain. I don't know much about breaks in legs but it appears to me this one was quite severe. As usual he does not attempt to fill me in on anything, expecting me to blindly fill his needs. His manner is surly, and his bad temper is always simmering just below the surface. Fortunately he cannot move too well and his threats remain just that, threats. He is rude and boorish, with all the pleasantness of a chained bear.

We have a major issue with the shower. His home is totally unsuitable for his recovery because of the bathroom. The shower is perched over a tub and he cannot shower easily. I am most fearful he will fall. Even his brother got into an argument with him over this and it was not pretty. I had not yet seen these two men fight, and the verbal exchanges were extremely colorful and heated. Master won out though, and still stubbornly persists to stay in his home.

It seems the angrier he gets the more his sex drive grows. What is more disturbing last night his sex failed him, something I have never witnessed in all the four years I have known him. Obviously it was a shock to him also. He pushed me from him hurting himself in the process and told me to leave. I hid in the bedroom finally falling asleep in the bed. It was the best night's sleep I have had in over a week.

I lay in bed in the darkness, Master asleep in his chair, he was still in pain and it was too difficult for him to rest comfortably in the bed. He had sent me away often of late, no longer seeming to require I sleep at his feet. Since his failure to perform he had put the chastity belt on me, and it has not come off.

I lay awake this night missing the warm comfort of the man who shared this bed and my mind was wandering with many thoughts, not all of them pleasing or restful. Everyone had their own choice of poison, and I wondered if mine was the pursuit of strong men? Some people like my mother took tranquilizers, my father chain smoked, Mick, heavier drugs of the illegal kind. Master's choice of poison had always been alcohol. I can understand his injury had demoralized him, and for a proud self reliant man it is a hard cross to bear. He felt his brother was his keeper as he brought us groceries and ran Master's errands. I wished I could have been more useful, but I had never learned to drive, it's not that I had not wanted to but Master himself had blatantly insisted I did not need to. Living under his roof and rules I did as I was told.

I felt in my limited capacity as nursemaid nothing more than a burden, and I was concerned that Master's parents either did not know he had been hurt, or even worse did not care. I began to wonder if he was somehow estranged from the rest of his family, or had he chosen to sever the link? He was indeed a puzzling enigma to me. I so wanted to know his stories and history. The bills seemed to get paid, and there was food on the table, though I could sense he was stressed to be laid off so long from work. However I dared not broach any of this with him, he was not a man to let me in on any of his fears if indeed he had them.

He was supposed to eat well I know that much, it's important in anyone's recovery. I had tried to make sure he did just that, but instead he seemed to eat only little, and he has taken up drinking heavily. I am worried and I know his brother is as well. He spends many of the evenings here by Master's side, sleeping on the couch or sometimes in the spare room. More unusually he has never asked to touch me or even tried, I guess he and Master did have words and I am for the time being off limits? I was grateful I did not have to wrestle with him during all this. Master's issues are proving more than enough.

HE WHO HATES

Most of the past few days has been quiet. I fetch, I carry, I try to please him in every way. My father had always told me when I was growing up that his home was his castle and that a man should be respected as the King of it by all those who lived under his roof, and all who visited his sanctum as well. I have lived by that saying my entire life and I try to please Master with all my heart.

Master's brother visits us when he can in-between his work schedule. He all but lives here at the moment. The television is on non stop I can hear it from every room, its the background sound to my life at this moment. I live silently with my fears and my mixed feelings that teeter like a see saw between joy and fearfulness. I watch him consume bottle after bottle of drink while he presides in his chair. This cannot be helping his bones heal? He seems to have no issue taking pain medications with them, he just grins at me and tells me it makes them work all the better. I want to cry silent tears sequestered in the kitchen from his view, if only he would be better soon. Things here have been most subdued, it appears all the immediate world does truly revolve around the fortunes of this man, at least mine do.

I heard him up and about, it is hard for him to navigate this place on crutches. To that end I had cleared away anything that might make his life even more difficult than it already was. Cleo had been rushing about madly only moments before, the kitten still in her, she loved to play. Every fleeting shadow, every nook or cranny contained some imagined prey which she would pursue wildly. Sliding helter-skelter over the linoleum or clinging to the shabby carpets. Her wild games gave me much joy, but in recent days I found myself wishing she would feel as subdued as everyone else here. I could sense Master was annoyed by her.

The crashing sound was obscenely loud to my ears. I jumped, I had already registered that it was Master who had fallen, heavily. Not only had he fallen but I could hear splintering of wood, and worse still my poor cat's tortured meow. I ran from the kitchen to be greeted by the sight of him in an awkward heap in the centre of the room, the wooden coffee table top completely smashed and splintered. He looked at me, and I felt in that gaze as though he could have ordered hell to freeze over. Cleo the obvious cause of his fall was nowhere in sight, I wished I could have done the same. Master needed me I could not shirk my duty.

I approached him, he had not moved, it was obvious he was furious he had fallen, and angry with his body that refused to do his bidding. I am sure he was hurting too. Any words of comfort or reassurance I had died in my throat. "Where is that fucking cat?" His tone was deadly, sounding more like a mass murderer than the man I loved.

I did not reply I could find nothing at this moment I knew would appease him. I reached for his arm to help him stand recoiling as all he did was slap me. "You fucking useless little bitch!" He spat from his place on the floor. I could all but feel the vitriol and frustration emanating from him like some kind of poisonous cloud that infected us all. He did not attempt to stand, I could smell the scotch on his breath, but instead took out his aggression on the closest object, the sundered coffee table.

Master is a very strong man and when he is enraged even more so, I cowered on the floor as he destroyed all that remained of the unfortunate piece of furniture. His hands were bloody in his rage but he seemed not to notice, and he flung the sundered pieces all about the room breaking the lamp and crumbling the plaster from the walls. I dare not move, I held my hands over my head waiting for him to turn his focus toward me. I could hear nothing but his ragged breathing, and for the longest time I did not look up.

I do not know how long the two of us shared the floor of the room in that fashion but it seemed, at least to me a long while. I felt his bloodied hand wet and sticky on my shoulder and warily gazed up at him, he looked like a cornered lion. Proud, defensive, and vicious, one who would fight to the end. I just wanted him to get better.

In silence I helped him stand, he seemed shaken and out of sorts, but the anger had been channeled out of him. I helped him to the bathroom where I bathed his cuts and bandaged his hands, he leant on his crutches watching me numbly. In that moment I saw the fleeting glimpse of the young boy that he might have been once, long ago. Unsure, no longer full of ego or command, but mortal and fallible just like I was. I loved him all the more, for letting me see that boy hidden inside.

"You loved that cat more than me." Was all he said, his voice flat and toneless. I looked a the limp body of my tiny friend and wept heartfelt tears of grief and loss. I did not have to ask him what had happened, I already knew.

THE OTHER WOMAN

Perhaps it was a ruse to show me how he felt about me loving or caring for anything more than I did him. I am still not sure. However it was most difficult for me to get through nonetheless. It was late Sunday afternoon when I heard Master answer his cell phone. He does not get many calls, mostly just Mick and his brother, and he guards that phone diligently, it never leaves his person. He never said anything to me, but he did sound very delighted to be talking to the caller, perhaps it was some good news. God knows we needed some.

It was about an hour later when there was a knock at the door. Not the heavy handed thumping of a man, but a light impatient, rap. "Open it." Master commanded from his place. I walked towards the door wrapped in my blue blanket. "You won't be needing that, drop it." He instructed. I paused, but not long enough to raise his ire. I hoped he was sure I thought, as I did so. It would be most awkward to open the door naked to someone who would not suspect it. I put my hand on the door latch and opened it hesitantly. There she stood tall and proud..........Birgitte.

"About time." Was all she said as she pushed past me in the doorway, making her way over to Master and kissing him warmly. I stood stupidly in my nakedness, with only my steel badges of office to cover me.

"How was Italy?" He asked.

"Delightful." She purred.

Master rose awkwardly from his place and the two embraced, her hands wandering over his lean body. I could not bring myself to move. "I missed you." He said lustily and he kissed her on the mouth. Master looked at me across the room, and his smile was laden with sadistic self satisfied victory.

"Drinks bitch, have you forgotten your manners?" Waving me towards the kitchen and turning his full attention back to statuesque Birgitte. I did not know what to think or how to feel as I stumbled blindly into the kitchen. I wanted to weep but there were no tears. I was well beyond the feeling of utter desolation. I wanted nothing more than to just stay out of sight. I decided perhaps it was best if I brought refreshments and just went to Master's room.

I cast my eyes to the floor looking at my toes. I could hear them talking pleasantries and he telling her he had missed her, and she responding that she had been sorry she had been away while he was laid up. I set down the tray, and backed from the room. Only too glad to be gone from the sight of the magnificent man I would gladly lay down my life for. That very same man fawning on the woman who looked like a film star, but Master was wise to my exodus of stealth. "Where are you going slave? Did I ask you to leave?" Birgitte smiled smugly at my obvious distress her red lips curling in her trademark cruel smile. I could see her cherry lipstick on his face and bull neck, I felt sick.

"Stand right here." He pointed to the floor. I did as he requested, my mind numb.

"She's not very old is she?" Birgitte questioned.

"Nineteen in October." Master informed her.

Birgitte shook her head and laughed. "Ah you beast you like them young." She had her hand under his shirt on his broad back. "But honestly." She continued. "She's such a fumbling baby, not a real woman." The words flowed melodiously off her tongue like honey. "She could not please you like someone older, more confident in who she is." Her appraisal stung me more than any insult I had ever heard from a man's lips. I could do nothing more than look at the carpet willing myself into the little space I have learned to go in my mind when things get too rough.

They made me stand there, they made me witness their love making, it was fierce and beautiful. I felt abject and realized I was not like her, the bold lioness, and he the great lion. I was a cowed, simpering, piece of meat to him along side of her. I am dead inside. He behaved with her in ways I had never seen him behave, he deferred to her, he cared what she thought, she called the shots and he complied. She sat on his lap her short shirt hitched up, he was hard in her. She was pulling his hair and digging her long cherry colored nails into his hard flesh drawing blood. Something I would never do, and he was moaning in his unbridled pleasure.

I stood silently. I find I no longer feel ashamed of my naked body, nor for any to gaze on it. I have recently realized I am more ashamed of my demeanor and my mind. Master tore me from my special place deep inside with his often simple words. "Herover Myra." They had finished but Birgitte shamelessly smiled at me her skirt hitched up, her long shapely legs open, his essence dripping from her. Master grabbed my collar. "Now slave I want you to learn what it is to truly serve a real lady." He pushed my face between her legs, my nostrils full of the fishy female scent of her combined with the scent of him. She lay back and he watched as I cleaned the evidence of his love making from her thoroughly with my tongue.

I had been deeply humiliated, and when Master did finally give me my leave I ran to the bedroom and cried. Through my morass of self loathing and grief I vaguely heard the front door slam, the quilt that covered the pillows was sodden. I heard him come in, he was no longer silent with his clumsy cast and his crutches. I felt the bed tilt under his substantial weight as he sat. He stroked my hair. I was on my stomach my face buried in the covers. The worst of my crying over I could hear his words.

"Once there was a little girl who loved a cat, more than she loved me." He sighed, and resumed stroking my hair. "Yet the little cat did not give her all I have." He added wistfully. "Now you know Myra how much you hurt me, giving your love to something other than me. See how it feels? See how it wounds me?"

I could not believe he thought Cleo had in any way been a threat to him. I was dumbstruck. His possession chilled me to the bone. "I'm sorry." Was all I could choke out.

"It will not happen again Myra, you love me remember? Only me."

After Master's little interlude with the stunning Birgitte It seems he has rediscovered his lost libido. I am glad, he had me worried as well, but it saddens me the way he chose to do it. I do wonder who she really is to him. A lover, an old flame, or merely someone in on this twisted game? I want to ask, I want to plumb his deep mysteries. However his resolute silence holds me back, further fueled by my fear.

The days that have followed I find are sombre ones. Even spring cannot allay my melancholy. I have not felt like doing anything much, I sit, I read, I cannot concentrate and I look forlornly out the window. I miss her my little friend so full of life.............

<u>MICK'S GIRL</u>

A familiar song playing on the radio, until now I had never really listened to the lyrics of this song, today I found I did........

" You let me violate you........ You let me desecrate you.......... You let me penetrate you............... You let me complicate you."

My thoughts turn to Master and his blind savagery and possessive avarice, yes he has done all that to me, and more. The song said it all..........

"Help me, I broke apart my insides. Help me, I've got no soul to sell. "Help me, the only thing that works for me. Help me get away from myself. I want to fuck you like an animal................"

Disturbing, but those painful words described him perfectly and could sanctify his actions, and possibly mine. Was he as tortured as I? Perhaps he was, and that would explain to me many things. Were we just two people who could not begin to approach our dark extremes no matter what we did? I was afraid I was right.

It is late Friday and I had been told this morning as Master made to leave for a time with his brother, he was going to have Mick over for the weekend. It was hard to hold the disappointment and dread out of the set of my body. I could only mutter over and over in my mind, a slave must always be pleasing. If only it was so easy. The news cast a dark shade over my already sombre state. I so fear that man, he brings out all that is bad in Master without fail.

I am furtive these days with my computer time, it's hard to speak for very long with anyone. I never realized how much I enjoyed my alone time until now. Master's presence here is almost oppressive and I find I am only too happy to see him depart to give me some much needed breathing space.

She was so very different to me, overweight, bent and cowed, older. At first glance I spied the tell tale steel collar, not nearly so subtle as mine was. A flat band of one inch polished steel with a heavy metal O ring suspended from it. It told the world for all to witness what she represented to Mick. Her skin was white and soft, her mousy shoulder length hair straight and lank. She smiled at me, a rueful stolen smile, she was like me a sister in slavery and I acknowledged and respected her stoic courage.

Master was always happy to see his sadistic minded friend, his fellow brother in all things cruel. I shivered though it was far from cold and pulled my blanket tighter about me in an unconscious gesture. Mick ordered her to sit on the floor by the lounge. I did likewise by Master's chair ready to jump at any command. I found could not take my eyes from her, I know it is rude to stare but I could not help myself looking at this most unfortunate creature. Her milky skin was scarred in many places, and I found myself wondering how much more scarring could I not see beneath her clothing. Perhaps she was evidence Master was indeed merciful. I could not imagine her life and conditions with Mick, but I sensed they were harsh. She never once looked up from the floor though I am sure she sensed I was looking at her. Was Gabrielle like this I wondered, defeated by life, how could Master have given her to him?

I never learned her real name, Mick just called her Tubby, cruel but fitting, short and solid as she was. I had expected from the outset that it would be a trying weekend, but events did not progress as I had expected.

Master ordered pizza it was a very pleasant change from our usual fare, even I made quite a pig of myself. Master seemed not to notice or care, and I did wonder if his plans for me included anything sinister. However the evening progressed to be rather ordinary, with the two men idly talking and watching the television. Master sent me to the kitchen for the last coffee of the evening, and I was surprised to hear raised voices, it appeared the two friends were having an altercation.

"Why the hell not!" Mick spat, I could plainly hear the disappointment in his tone.

"Because I said so." Master snarled stubbornly from his chair.

"I'd share with you, you miserable cunt." Mick whined. Lighting another cigarette.

"If you didn't take drugs maybe I'd feel different, but I've said it before and I'll say it again you are not using her." It dawned on me as I stood there straining to hear the exchange, Master was absolutely unwilling to share me with this man. I guess he had told me the truth about the night of his party, and I felt much chagrined not to have believed him.

I so wanted to speak with her, but she was forbidden to talk, or look directly at anyone. She did not even attempt to try. Her blind obedience frighted me. I realized Master could if he chose to enforce the same fearful obedience on me as well. I watched Mick stub out his cigarettes on her arms she did not even pull away. Master just looked at Mick and grinned, I felt nauseated.

Apart from the specter of Tubby the weekend was decidedly tame. Her presence had a distinctly sobering effect on me though, and I realized a slave could not have limits, all she could cling to was hope. The simple hope that her Master would not choose to exceed more than she could bear.

"Would you do that to me?" I asked of him as I sat carefully on his lap Wednesday evening. I was ever mindful of his cast. He looked at me in a quizzical manner, I touched his golden stubbled jaw ever so lightly. He fascinated me, he was so different to me in every way. Even after all these years, and all of our trials and tribulations, he still took my breath away.
"What do you mean?" His jade eyes narrowed, his pupils were black pools.
"Like what Mick did to Tubby." I ventured carefully.

He shook his golden head. "No Myra." He looked at me. I was not sure if I registered disappointment there.

"Then why did you give Gabrielle to him?" It was something I had to have finality on, yet risky to speak of.

"Ah so that is what this is about is it, Gabrielle?" I nodded and lowered my eyes. "I was young Myra, not much older than you are now. I could not deal with a drug addict. She made my life hell Myra." He sighed. I tried to imagine any woman moving him in any manner and I could not. Nor could I fathom why he could not easily deal with her as he did me. "I can see my little Myra you do not understand, maybe one day I will take you to Amsterdam and you can see for yourself." I wondered how I would do this on an expired Visa.

"Mick understood her, he could supply her with her needs Myra. It got so bad here I could only lock her up. I built that cell in the basement because of it."

I tenderly ran my fingers through his wheaten hair. "Did he hurt her?"

"I'm sure he did Myra."

"Would you do that to me?"

"No Myra, no." His usually hard visage looked hurt. "I thought you might understand by now my little one. You are special, you are mine. You allow me to do the things I must do, special things I cannot do with anyone else."

I felt it was one of those rare moments, I had him cornered and I took a further risk. "What about Birgitte? What does she do?" He looked at me for some moments then cast his eyes out the window to the street beyond. I could see the cars parked on the curb reflected in his clear eyes. He took a deep breath and fidgeted in his chair, my weight meant nothing to him.

"She is not you Myra, she cannot be."

"But you loved her?"

"Yes, I did, but it is not the same............ Perhaps I am greedy but I need more than just one woman. I could not do to her the things I do to you Myra, and if I had to choose I would choose what you give me over everything." I did not know what to say.

The following day he presented me with a huge bouquet of red roses.

SAVAGE LOVE

It appears Master has now taken on the mission of siring new life with great zeal, his earlier lusts have returned in force, and it only takes the merest hint of flirtation to inflame his desire. Last night things were different to usual, I was told not to cook dinner. A command that never fails to lead me to anxiety. I fretted all day pacing the worn carpet here until his return.

Finally, the sound of his car pulling up to the curb. He should not drive with his broken leg but he does. I knelt by the door, the fresh spring air touching my skin in a gentle caress as he opened it to stand for some time examining me, perched on his crutches. "Very beautiful slave." His voice was imbued with lust. I could smell delicious aroma of food, my favorite Chinese. He had seen fit to treat me this evening, a rare occurrence indeed.

We ate informally on the new coffee table. I was not sure it had been a good idea to purchase a glass topped piece, after the demise of that last one. However it was his home and his choice, something I have very little say in.

The light this time of year is beginning to draw out, Master tells me that during summer here the days are very long, some seventeen hours of sunlight. I find that hard to imagine. He also informed me it can begin to get light as early three in the morning during the months of high summer. These golden people, in the land of winter darkness seem to have a huge love of the sun, and I pray Master will allow me to enjoy it this summer.

Dinner over I cleared away the remnants of the meal. It was a delight to not have to clean up. I could hear children playing in the quiet street, and the chortling of birds, as they made to roost in the great tree in the back yard, which was now burgeoning in a cloak of vital greenery. He was drawing the curtains, but he did not close the windows. Master was clumsy with his cast, I had grown used to his noisy approach and was comforted by the fact he could not soundlessly observe my actions, nor surprise me easily. I am sure it annoyed him, he liked nothing more than to catch me off guard.

As I have said I never wear clothing in his presence unless specifically instructed. Master is not a man for trifles and triviality. He does not need lingerie nor make up to excite him. Just me as I was created. This fine evening was no different. I stood before him with only his cold, unbending steel on my person, he appraised me head to toe very slowly, lingering at the places on my body that most delighted him. Even after all these years I find I must look away from his assessing, animal gaze.

He placed his finger gently under my collar and pulled me forward, so very close to him. When he does this seemingly very ordinary thing, and he does it often, I feel the most shameful things in places deep inside. I know I already want him to do so many forbidden things. I never voice my carnal requests, he already knows they are there, and what they are. He takes off the chastity belt, its constricting heaviness leaves my body and I feel free. He sits in his chair, his cast hinders him a little in his love making, diminishing the possibilities we once had.

I made to climb into his lap but surprisingly he tells me to go to the kitchen and lie on the table. My excitement is now tempered by fear, activities in the kitchen are, I have learned often to be feared. However I do as I am told, I have no desire to anger him. The table is cold on my back. I lay there my legs drawn up and wait for him. His hands are empty and I relax a little, I had expected rope. He pulls up a chair and sits awkwardly between my upraised legs. I still feel most self conscious, strange really as my shame over my body should be gone long ago. He studies my privates for some time. He does not move or speak.

The old chrome chair creaks on the linoleum as he stands, his hands hot and heavy stray to my nipples. I jump as he pinches them sending tingling sensations of desire to the core of my very being. His thick golden hair brushes my stomach, vibrant green eyes lingering as his lips kiss his mark there, his unshaven chin prickling my sensitive skin.

He lapses into Danish phrases in his passion, I catch some of his meaning but not all. I lay passive and let him do as he wishes. He again sits on the chair, his leg is awkward for him. On this May evening he does something he rarely does, kissing me lower and lower until he is caressing my femaleness with his tongue and his teeth. Small squeals escape my lips, I wriggle on the table top lost in what he can do to me. The first time he ever did this I was only fifteen. I wanted to die, the feelings so intense and unbridled. I had no idea a man could do this to me. He is right he makes me his slave with such little effort, in only minutes I am panting and moaning wildly as he toys with my receptive body. He can play me like an instrument, and in his hands I feel that is all I am.

I ached for him, I wanted him more than anything at this moment. He toyed with me taking his time. Inciting my desires and making me beg for his attention. "What are you Myra?" He said thickly.

"Your slave Sir?" I moaned. His fingers were in me but I wanted more, much more. I pushed into them, he withdrew.

"No Myra what are you?" He patiently repeated.

"I am yours Sir, I exist only for you. Your slave, your slut, your whore." I all but cried in my desperation.

"Yes, you are." He whispered in my ear seductively. "If I wanted to Myra I could do anything I liked, anything at all........" His large hands went to my throat, I froze and he laughed. A low menacing chuckle, my desire had receded swiftly as I sensed the seeds of danger. "No one knows you are here Myra, you my little girl do not exist."

His hands tightened on my airway, and I found my own hands trying to pull his fingers from my throat, in a gesture of futility. He was above me now as I lay prone on the table top, his eyes glinting with inherent evil. Steadily he applied pressure, he had done this to me many times before while we made love. However tonight he was different, and the undercurrent of fear tore at my sensibilities. At times he could be the most changeable man, and I had wondered if perhaps he possessed split personalities. So many people had told me was a monster, a criminal, and he would hurt me gravely one day, or God forbid, even kill. He could kill I knew that, the little grave in the back yard was testament to the ugly truth.

"You see Myra if I can't have you no one can." He spoke softly in a voice that seemed almost not his own. "I am torn little one, but I will not give you to Mick, you are mine or you are no ones."

His grip was steadily shutting off my air, lightheaded and gasping for breath, I found I had no voice to plead him to stop. My hands were on his, attempting to vainly wrest his fingers from my throat. I began to kick at him blindly with little care for the consequence of my actions. One hand left my neck but the other never strayed. Even when I registered he had removed the much feared belt from his waist, I continued to lash out at him fiercely. I felt the stinging slap on my behind, the crack of the leather on my flesh resoundingly loud. The blinding pain pulled me up, he had hit me much harder than usual. He raised the strap to strike me again and I froze, again his low wicked laugh, he sounded unbalanced. It chilled me to hear him, but he did not strike me again.

Hand firmly entwined in the back of my hair he pulled me up like I was a doll, wrapping the belt about my throat. He pulled it tight, I dare not utter the one word I so wanted to, the one he never liked to hear. I could sense he was waiting for it to tumble carelessly from my mouth, and give him the excuse he needed for more needless cruelty. He pushed me back on to the table the height was comfortable for him, again he pushed his fingers in me roughly. His other hand holding the constrictive leather strap on my neck, it was very tight.

"You want it don't you bitch." I nodded an affirmative, realizing I did. He pulled me towards him, I felt like a hunk of meat. I needed more air than he would allow, I felt faint and so hot. His invading fingers did not relent. I found I kept pushing toward him in my hunger to be sated, he never satisfied it more than partially. The belt was becoming ever tighter as I pulled against it in my need. "How much do you want it Myra?"

I could not answer I could barely function at all, and somewhere in my inner conscience I could not believe the things he made me feel. I was alive, so very much alive. I whimpered as he withdrew his teasing pleasure and risked tightening the belt even tighter to get nearer to him, the waves of my desire now so great. He was hard, his jeans unzipped as he stood at the head of the table. To my bewilderment he just leant over me looked me in the eye and masturbated until he came all over my stomach.

"Remember slave it's not about you and your pleasure, it's about mine." He let go of the belt and slapped me across the face. "Never forget it."

In the early hours of the morning I lay awake pondering the lesson of the evening before. I was sleepless with unquenched, burning, desire gnawing at me. He often left me like this to suffer in silence at nights, so close to him almost whimpering to be sated. His cryptic words echoed in my head, what did he mean he was torn? Torn by what? I did not understand.

My mother once told me you cannot know a man until you live with him. I find myself often reviewing her words that seemed so cliché and old. Perhaps she was right, and then again I look at the man I live with and feel perhaps she was not. Do I know him, physically yes, but his mind, no I fear I do not? He is a mystery, an enigma to me, yet he knows and uses all I am. However my one secret I will not divulge, the last bastion of the intellectual and still vibrant Myra; my writings here.

I long to understand his words of last evening, though it would have been playing with fire to press him for the answer. Hard and obdurate as he is I sense something of import is weighing heavily on his soul, and I have no clues as to what it is. I fear it will have a profound effect on the terms of my slavery. I do hope I am wrong; trust, I tell myself it's about laying back and trusting him to do what is best.

NASCENT LIFE

It is a beautiful golden evening as I write this, the birds sing in the greenery outside, the last of the slanting sun's rays are golden and pure, as they pierce through the windows making all they touch seem more than it truly is. This rare moment when the quality of the light is the kind a photographer waits all day for, only to find it gone in but passing moments if he is unprepared. Yes, so pure, so beauteous, unlike my abhorrent thoughts and lies. I have wronged him, it gnaws at me. I know it is my duty to disclose my condition, he will see it soon and hard questions will follow. However it is also my deeper duty to keep that which passes between us a private accord. Yes, I have failed him, I am weak and I despise myself. I deserve all and more he could inflict on me.

Of late Master often stays out to the early hours at Mick's tattoo parlor, this activity is not at all unusual, he often does this as he cannot work at least in manual endeavors with his cast. Less than two weeks until it is at last removed. I will be glad as it irritates his already short temper just by its existence. If it is not Mick's company he courts late he is up to the small hours here on this computer that houses my secrets, and those of his he unwittingly shares with an audience. He would be beyond fury if he knew of my betrayal; guilt fills my entire being as I serve him in silence as he does his father's books. So many large sums of money he works with I am at last beginning to understand the magnitude of his family's company and its vast holdings. There is so much more to him I do not know, he never spoke to me of this nor any of his familial business matters. I am a slave, nothing more.

I feel very tense right now. I sense Master knows I am up to no good, not sure he knows how, but he senses deception like a wolf would sense it. He is more animal than man. I can admire that honesty. However it does not help my cause. For my own peace of mind and safety I decided reluctantly to no longer visit the computer or my journal on line for a time. In this time I will attempt to tell my Master of the child I know I will have this winter, the child that is not his but that of his brother. I hope he takes it well.

All week I have sat looking at him ever so subtly gauging his mood, will he be receptive to my news, I so wish to impart to him. I watch him guardedly in the evenings drinking his black coffee, or much harder beverages, mostly he sits in his chair enthroned like a king, unmoving. Even in his partially inebriated state I still cannot find the words nor the courage to tell him my few simple woes. One small utterance and it would be relieved, all the duplicities revealed, gone and hopefully assuaged. I do not blame him for what has happened, I only feel blame focussed firmly on myself. It is I who have erred. He is the Master he knows what is best, and I have like a fool sought to undermine him.

Seven days I have been strong, the time has dragged by, without my crutch to lean on and my few tentative contacts with the outside world to converse with. I live in a wretched state of nervousness and guilt. I keep waiting for him to question me, to call me to him in that tone of voice that brooks no refusal. That very same mode of voice that makes me tremble, and want him all in one. However he does not, he just meets my fleeting gaze staring back at me boldly. Is he enjoying what he knows is my internal misery, or is he oblivious to it? There is no way to tell, it is maddening.

In those seven days not one utterance from me of any form of confession, nature will soon intervene and he will be wise to the child I carry. Perhaps he will not care if it is he, or his brother who sired it. Sometimes I wonder if he did not plan it all along. I know I can never tell of my journal and my writings it is madness, but there is a rebellious part of me that wants to so I can feel better, to be somehow absolved and descend into slavery in all finality. So many things I fight, and I realize the worst argument one can have is that of inner turmoil. I clutch so many demons to my breast, my reality is slipping and it is a fearsome thing.

Today before Master left to get his cast removed at long last, he made the comment I was putting on weight. As he struggled to fasten the chastity belt. I had to confess it fit more snugly in recent days than it had in the past. I think I know why but I am afraid to tell him my fears.

As I lay in bed last evening I could feel this warm feeling in my lower belly where my womb is. It's hard to describe it's like a pleasing, warm, humming sensation. I have to be very still and lay in the dark to really feel it there. I put my hands over it but I can feel no difference on the outside. I have no experience to base this on but I think I may be with child.

It was strange to see Master return without his cumbersome cast. I am sure he was very relieved to see it finally removed. In recent days it had been bothering him immensely, it itched in places he could not scratch, and had begun to put pressure on his leg. As always I did my best to comfort him. He is far from fully recovered though. I overheard him speaking with his brother last evening, it will still be many weeks, possibly months before he can resume his full workload. It is most fortunate he works for his father's construction company. I do not believe he is pressed for money, I get the sense he has a substantial amount of liquid capital at his disposal. He just chooses to live simply. Probably very wise in this downturn of the world economy.

He is reliant on his crutches every now and then, and tires easily. I can see it frustrates him, like everything he does he expects immediate results. However he will be resuming work this Wednesday, doing as he explained light duties in the office. I think he was happy to at least be doing something after all these weeks cloistered at home. I can identify with that sentiment.

I'm afraid now, today without warning I became suddenly ill. One minute I was fine, the next I was retching miserably into the toilet. Master stood watching my distress leaning on his crutches in the bathroom doorway. "Its not like you girl to be sick." He gazed at me questioningly. I washed my face in the cool water over the sink and rinsed my mouth. At least I felt a lot better, if only physically.

"I'm okay." I tried to assure him. He still stood there and I figured that perhaps he might have wished me to leave so that he could use the bathroom. He often watched me, but I was forbidden to impinge on his privacy.

I made to leave, and attempted to pass him in the doorway, but he blocked my exit. His large body effectively filling the portal. He did not say a word but lay his hand on my belly. "It's not mine. Is it?" He said quietly. I really was unsure, but the timing did not bode well. I did fear it was his brothers.

"I really don't know." I answered in a cracked whisper. Because in truth I did not.

That evening Master returned with a pregnancy test kit, he placed it on the table in the kitchen. Heartlessly he said. "Lets see if the bitch is in pup." He followed me to the bathroom and made me procure for him a urine sample. He did the test himself, frowning at the result. "Hum.......... Well, it appears you are." I burst into tears.

CHANGE OF HEART

"As it is likely not mine, but my brothers we need to get rid of it." He said callously. I looked at him but did not answer. I was of two minds. This was a baby, my baby. Part of me agreed with him, not for his selfish reasons, but my own very different ones. I was scared I had to admit, I did not feel we had a suitable living environment to raise a child in, nor did I feel I was remotely ready. No matter who fathered this child I held within, this baby was still of my flesh, it could only be Master's or his brother's. There had been no one else. Worst case scenario it was his brother's child, they were so alike no one would ever know any different.

Other fears had crept into my conscience as well, enhanced by the death of my cat. Having a baby, would it make any difference to this often violent, changeable man? I suspected not, though I had seen a baby change many things. I felt sick with the choice I had to make.

The guilt and fear eat at me and I hope that no woman has to do what I must this day. I know it is for the best, yet deep inside I feel it is most wrong. I cannot believe my first excursion into the outside world will be to an abortion clinic. I look at the clock. I have been watching it methodically count down the hours until his return so he may escort me there. I was advised on the phone by a very understanding lady while Master hovered close by, they will do nothing today. They merely want to see me and discover if I am indeed pregnant. I then get to dwell on what I want to do for twenty-four hours before I can return and make my dreadful decision. Oh torture, Master could not have thought of anything more painful if he had tried.

My first trip outside the walls and I was crying so hard I did not look at a thing. I do not even know where we went, I was past caring. He did not speak to me nor offer me any comfort. Master did not seem affected by this as I was. He escorted me inside, I know he will give me no out on this. Graven faced he helped me fill in all the forms. I was too teary to write and read, I was asked of course if this was of my own free will? I did my best to smile wanly and say yes, looking as sincere as I could muster in the circumstance.

I'm sure they see many women like me caught between unfortunate extremes. Master stood close by I could tell he was nervous for they would not let him accompany me for the whole procedure, he was afraid I would crumble and tell all. I saw the way the staff looked at him too, I think they knew exactly what he was, or maybe to them men were all such fiends. It was, even in my grief interesting to see him so uncomfortable.

I was told I was about eight weeks or so. I gazed on the image my tiny baby, just a little black jelly bean on the ultrasound screen. It was there, it was real, it was mine. The only thing that was truly mine, but was it, even this he could dictate. It was a crystalizing moment.

That evening when we returned home Master was most silent, perhaps today had affected him more than I realized. Was he having second thoughts? I know I was.

After a wordless, unappealing, dinner he sat me on his knee in the kitchen, he looked at me long and hard, holding my face cupped in his large rough hands. "It's hard Myra but its for the best, it's not mine."

"Yes," Was all I could bring myself to answer, ashamed I had no fight in the face of his lordly presence. The wet of my tears already spilling on to his hands and running down my cheeks. He was right this was his brother's child, and I wonder if he had even told him. I suspected he had not. This life I carried within was doomed from the first.

"It cannot be, my slave not this time." His voice was deep, and unusually expressive. I wondered what he meant by that? I did hope he did not have this in store for me again any time soon.

"I don't think I am ready for children you are right." I had to agree I did not think he was, he was going to make sure I did this terrible thing tomorrow. There was going to be no reprieve.

Back to the clinic again, more crying and recriminations. I saw the Doctor, and like everyone else there she too was a lovely woman and made me feel at ease. She explained to me what was to happen and as I had found out early I could simply take a pill and it would not be at all invasive, unlike if I had left it a lot longer. Unless of course there was complications, but as she said they were somewhat rare. I was glad, this was hard enough as it was.

One pill, it was yellow. Such a happy color I mused as she placed it in my hand, I took a deep breath and swallowed it down, it was done. The Doctor took great pains to tell me this pill had terminated the baby, and that I must use without fail the other pill to make sure it aborted properly. I nodded and assured her I would do just as she had instructed.

I walked from the clinic with Master by my side, his hand sought mine. I looked at him and he looked down at me, something strong passed between us, wordless yet powerful. I felt a rush of relief and realized I had done the correct thing. I even looked around a little on the way home, for once in many weeks my head was held high.

Thursday evening Master made gentle love to me, a rarity for him but I do treasure these beautiful moments we do share. Then when he had finished he pushed the remaining pill inside of me, and told me to lay down and rest. It did not take very long to work, a mere hour or so. I had been told to expect the worst, severe cramping and nausea, but the effects were very mild. Nothing more than a heavy period. My baby was gone, I cannot help wondering what he or she may have been. My biggest regret.

THE DARKEST THINGS

I was not ready for the shock of Saturday evening, it was not supposed to happen like this, I was assured. We were in the shower, I had been very agitated all day. I assumed my feelings were brought about by the effects of the abortion. My emotions were like a wild roller coaster. One moment I felt so vindicated, the next abject. I was enjoying the warm water and trying my best to relax, he was holding me close caressing and gentle, and I enjoying his nearness. I felt odd in a way I cannot explain, and before I understood what had happened I realized I had pushed something hard and quite sizable out of myself into the bath.

We both looked down at almost the same moment. It was unmistakable what I was looking at, my unborn baby. I was faster than he was. I already had it in the palm of my hand. I was face to face with the child I had held within, the little innocent being I had murdered. My utterance on seeing this was loud and inhuman I held it close to me clasped to my chest and completely lost myself in my grief. He prized it from my grasp and left me in the water to cry while he got rid of it. I will never forget it, never.

Today I sit, I have no energy for anything and will only post this and leave. I have no words to type other than these today. Nor can I bring myself to converse with anyone. Maybe tomorrow I will feel better?

This week has been a hard one I feel hollow, dead, and worn. Simple tasks require much effort. I take quiet solace in merely serving him. All I see is the little red creature on the floor of the bathtub, over and over. My little baby I failed you. I should not be here to write of this, my grief is deep, my sorrow endless. How did I fail?

I am a murderess, wretched and despised, the most despicable of all beings. I now heed the words of a fellow sister in slavery. 'I did not question my obedience until it cost a price.' As mine now has, and I cannot live with what I have done.

It is late afternoon there is plenty of time. I have elected to leave no departing note. I will not condemn him, nor acquit him in any form. I have naught to impart to my family. The bath tub is full of inviting almost too hot to be comfortable water, but I do not wish it to become cold, at least not yet. Master had conveniently provided me with my means for this out, and I am ready to take it. I fumble with the bottle of sleeping pills that he had been prescribed for the worst of the nights to ease his broken leg; but he had never taken. I am glad, for today I need them more than he. I am unsure if I should take them yet, or at all. I know this is the coward's way out, and I want for more than that. I seek the razor blades in the rear of the cabinet as his straight blade I cannot locate. They are clean and sharp, I run my fingers along their keen edges and they readily prick my skin. They will have to suffice.

Everything is ready, I ease into the bath. It is so hot it is difficult to sit down. I make myself, it will not matter shortly. I press the blade to my soft skin of my inner arm, thinking of Josh the boy at school who did the very same thing in his bedroom, minus the soothing luxury of the warm water. He was the weird all too thin Goth boy, always dressed in black, different to the rest. He seemed perpetually shrouded in melancholy. I sensed he was fighting more than just simple issues, and was not surprised to hear of his suicide. He was fifteen.

Josh was braver than I. I cut myself a little, but could not find the will to do a decent job of it. I set the blade down, suicide seemed so hard. I could so callously kill my baby, but not myself. It was an injustice. The thought lent me new resolve and I downed the pills and resumed my work with the blade. Two long cuts delivered with all the self hatred I could muster. I felt nauseous looking at my blood swiftly coloring the bath water, or was it the pills beginning to work so soon? I was unsure. I lay back looking at the ugly discolored ceiling, and the bare light bulb. This my last vision of earth? So ordinary, my eyes closed..........

I felt hands on me, wrenching me from the water. His hands...........

I woke in the bedroom, disoriented. I shouldn't still be here. I felt weak and light, a mere husk of a human being. I had failed even at this. He was there sitting beside me like a golden sentinel. My arms lay to my sides bandaged in clean white wrappings. I could see pin points of crimson on them. He stroked my hair saying nothing, he kissed my forehead. It was morning, and the day unusually bright. I had no words, nothing could ease my sense of failure, and thankfully perhaps he did understand silence was all I wished.

He sat with me a long time drinking coffee, the smell bothered my delicate and sore stomach. Neither of us said a word. I was content to lay unmoving and listen to the distant sounds of others, people who were not like us. He eventually conveyed to me in quiet words what happened. He had come home early. Pure chance, they had completed the job, and there was no more to do for the day. He had discovered me on the verge of passing out in the tub, and made me vomit up the pills. I think I vaguely remember this, but my recollection is dim. He told me the cuts were superficial, they would not have killed me. Though he said he had sutured them in places where they did run deep. He had not taken me to hospital but nursed me here. Given the fact I had outstayed my visa I was not surprised.

I wanted to cry, but I had no tears. Of all my most miserable failings this was the worst. He made me drink but I did not want to, the water seemed alien as it tricked down my throat, it was difficult to swallow.

"This place is not good for you Myra, I can see that now. It is my failing. Yes, I have failed you." He seemed genuinely sorrowful. I did not understand his words, he had failed me how? He had been all he promised and more, it was I who had failed. "I have decided we will sell this house, I will buy a bigger, better one. Perhaps move out to Arhas near the sea, I know you would like that. Things will be better my love you will see."

My love, an endearment I had never heard him utter, did he mean it? Had I even heard correctly? "I know I am a cruel man, yes I am guilty." He went on. "In my desire to make you my perfect slave I pushed you beyond what you could take. Yes, I have." He shook his shaggy head admonishing himself. "I don't want you to become as she did."

I assumed he was speaking of Gabrielle the addict girl who got too much. I just lay back and let him talk, he was gently stroking my face and looking at me. He spoke of her, his first real slave. He spoke of how he began to fear where he had pushed her, and of how he had not learned from his mistake in his treatment of me. He kept telling me she and I were different, and most remarkably his admission he was sorry. This was new to me, I had never heard him admit he was sorry in any form to me before. I did not know what to think, nor how to respond.

We spent the afternoon laying on the bed, his warm body close to mine. He had drawn back the curtains and the bright sunlight entered the room, the light summer breeze wafting through the gauzy curtains. The beautiful day a direct affront to where I wanted to be, dead in the dark and cold.

He nursed me back to health over the next few days, he took time off from work and watched me incessantly, and true to his word put his home up for sale the very next day.

I took the bandages off today, unwrapping them slowly coming face to face with my own act of self hatred. The red angry slashes were longer than I remembered, and I can see they will leave scars as indelible as his mark is on my flesh, and his slavery has been on my soul. In my shame I am not sure I will be able to again wear short sleeves in public, and possibly not at all.

My stitched wrists are tender as I attempt to type rubbing on the desk's edge. Master resumed work on Wednesday, I could tell he was very hesitant to leave me here alone. He made me swear I would be good and not harm myself again. He knows I am a creature of my word, he binds me with it, and I too know the insanity of the moment has passed. Yet I feel bereft, the summer world for me at least is filled with only shades of grey.

DIAMONDS ARE NOT FOREVER

Housework, yes it is one of my compulsions made even more so by Master's untidy habits, and the fact the house is now up for sale. I had begun to clean even places I had previously overlooked before. Today's messy subject was the bottom of the wardrobe. Master is one of those men who can just put something away and forget its existence. No matter how messy it is if he closes the door on it, it is quite forgotten. As I was doing this and attempting to make some order of his possessions I discovered on the set of drawers in his wardrobe a ring box. It was red velvet and looked very new. I opened it and almost dropped the box when I sighted its contents. Contained within was the most beautiful and expensive ring I had ever seen, something a film star would wear.

Gingerly I removed it from its crimson velvet bed. It was heavy white gold, the band half an inch in width. They had to be real diamonds. I wanted to scratch the glass with them to be sure, but was too afraid. There was one very large central rectangular stone with two matching ones set either side. The rest of the substantial band was inset with them also, it was the most beautiful thing. My thoughts returned to the day Master had given me the silver ring with the bluebird on it, I could not imagine being given something like this. Instinctively I knew this was probably worth more than my father's car. I slipped it on to my wedding finger feeling great disappointment, it was way too big for me, and on further observation it did not fit on any of my fingers. I could not imagine a man would buy a ring like this and not have it fit perfectly, it made no sense.

The sinking thought came to me then, he did not buy this for me.......................

Thursday afternoon Master came home very early, he had ordered me on parting that morning to iron his best shirt. I hate ironing and rarely do any, I don't even believe I am remotely good at it. However though inexperienced I did it to the best of my ability, looking at it long before deciding the garment would be up to his standard.

He breezed past me in the doorway, not acknowledging me at all. I did not move from my place, and he went straight to the bathroom. I was torn, but he had not given me permission to rise. I waited, he showered, emerging from the bathroom, towel about his waist; water droplets still beading on his flesh. He did not give me so much as a glance, nor did he free me from my post. He was a long time in the bedroom, he never took this long to dress. When he did emerge I could hardly recognize him as the man I knew. Removed from his usual blue collar attire Master looked like a celebrity. Black suit well cut, stark white shirt I had so carefully ironed, a tie about his bull neck. I did not know this man. He collected his car keys, wallet, and phone, patted me under the chin and told me to be good. The door slammed, I heard the keys in the lock, and he was gone.

This evening I sit alone, I have some music on for ambience, and the computer for solace. I would give almost anything to see what he is doing at this moment.

He sat silent in the kitchen, it was late, well after midnight. Again he passed me in the doorway, I could smell perfume on him mixed with his aftershave, he never looked at me. He simply went to the kitchen and sat in the dark. I felt very afraid.

Master can have an overbearing melancholy about him when one of his black moods strikes. Its so oppressive I feel I am being buried alive. I have not seen him this way since he fell, that dreadful day that sealed little Cleo's demise. I long to go to him, comfort him in his blackness, but I do not dare. Instead I sit quietly hoping he will call to me, but he does not.

One o'clock passes neither of us has moved, the music is still quietly playing in the background. My knees are beginning to bother me, but not as much as his brooding silence is. I wait yet another hour, my body now equally as uncomfortable as my mind is, finally making my decision for ill or good to retreat to the bed alone.

Friday morning I wake, it is still early, his absence in the bed disturbing. He should be at work, however I know today he will not be. I creep from the covers pulling my blanket about me, I feel like I am approaching a wounded lion in his den. He is still there, asleep on the table top, his long hair the color of a wheat field in high summer cascading over its dented surface, and set before him is the little red, velvet box.

Perhaps he will like some coffee? I know it is most important I try to assuage his hurt. I am fairly sure I understand what has happened, he is a man who does not take refusal well. That woman he has fallen for Brigitte, is a creature so like himself, cold, cruel, and heartless, and today he feels what he so routinely without thought, does to others. I want to feel pity, though even I feel a sense of appropriate justice has been done.

My industriousness in the kitchen slowly rouses him. I try not to look as he wakes and tucks the ring box sheepishly into his jacket pocket, yet we both know he has. I long to tell him I love him, because in spite of everything, I do, so very, very much. I place the coffee before him, it is strong and black, with spoonfuls of sugar. He drinks it slowly, with not a word for me. I sit at his feet, he slowly drinks looking about the room. For all his sartorial splendor he appears the king who has lost his crown.

The day was spent in mutual silence, I know Master well after all these years, making speech unnecessary between us to fulfill his wishes. Later that evening Master's brother arrived, I guess in his unscheduled absence at work this day his brother sensed trouble. I served them both dinner and retreated from the kitchen to let them talk. It was bad of me, but I so wanted to know all the juicy details. So I hovered nearby straining for every word.

"She'll hurt you Bro."

"I want her Svend." Master's voice was raw with emotion. "She understands me, she knows who I am."

Master's brother shook his head. "I've seen her kind, she will chew you up and spit you out. She's beautiful, but not worth it."

"What would you know!" Master spat.

"You can't afford her brother."

"Don't tell me what I can't afford!" Master was indignant now.

The elder man made a sound of frustration as he poured another drink. "Well, she refused your ring didn't she? Most women would have been all over you if you had of presented them with that. Think! She is chasing millionaires all over Europe. You are going down a sorry path brother, be satisfied with what you have." I knew he was referring to me.

Master made an exasperated, strangled sound, and the glass he was drinking from crashed to the floor as he angrily swiped his arm across the table top. His stalwart brother did not flinch, he was used to his younger siblings temper tantrums. He calmly poured another drink. "If you think she's so fucking fabulous why don't you just take her?" Master yelled without warning. He rose from the table abruptly, the bottle of scotch teetered dangerously, before miraculously righting its self. I jumped as he strode purposely into the lounge, grabbing me by my collar and hauling me into the kitchen before his brother, who was still calmly sitting at the table. "Take her! Go on, fucking take her! Thats what you want isn't it!" He thrust me roughly at Svend and went into the bedroom. I stood there awkwardly, his brother's cool grey eyes on me as we both listened to the bedroom being torn apart.

Some minutes later he emerged with a bag, which I presume was packed with my belongings. I did not have many. He threw some clothes in my direction, snarling at me to put them on. "I don't care what you do with her, get her out of my sight!"

I saw his brother hesitate. I thought for a moment they might actually come to blows, he looked gravely at Master, put his half finished drink down looking at me as I clumsily dressed. I could not believe Master would truly send me away. I was already teary eyed.

I felt a touch on my arm, fleeting gentle. Master took the entire bottle of scotch and upended it, he drank deeply looking at his brother in open defiance. "Nobody, including you, tells me what to do. Now get out!" Again the gentle urging touch, his brother was guiding me to the door, the door I had rarely stepped through in all these long months, out into the lingering summer twilight. Master never even watched us leave. As we drove away I looked back, the front door stood ajar.

Master's brother had a very lovely car, much nicer than any car I had ever had the privilege to ride in, it was a new Audi A6, black and shiny with leather interior. He was silent as he drove, he put on the radio. I looked out the window at the streets and buildings as we left Copenhagen. It was a long drive to his brother's home, some three hours. We crossed an immense bridge I could not believe the length of it, and we did not get to our final destination, Arhus until dark.

The homes in this area were expansive and beautifully maintained. Quiet streets, green lawns, and manicured gardens. I could see why Master had suggested we come here. I had often wondered what it might be like as a girl to live in a place like this? The automatic garage door gaped wide and we drove into it's dark maw. He grabbed my few belongings and escorted me inside. His home was beautiful and spacious, it appeared he lived alone. However unlike Master his domicile was very orderly and clean. There were vast areas of pristine, shining hardwood floors, and the carpets were white. One could see this had at one time been a loving couple's home. Pictures of her were everywhere. She was golden and beautiful, her image smiled back at me, from the mantles, the book shelves, and his great mahogany desk in his study, as I passed by, following him like a small, lost, child as he showed me where everything was. "My home is your home." Was all he said.

He deposited my bag in the master bedroom leaving me with no doubt what my duties to him would be. I could not hate this man, yet he was not the man I loved.

It was late. I was tired, more tired than I had realized, it had been a trying day. He was not ready for bed, he poured some white wine for us both in some thin crystal glasses. He even made me laugh as he made his glass sing as he rubbed the edges of it. I felt like a little girl in his presence, and I am sure that is how I appeared to him, some twenty years older I was. I squirmed with guilt when I thought of what I had done to his baby, he could never know.

I was struggling to drink my wine, I have never liked it, and it was making me even more weary. He put his hand on my hand, and I realized he still wore his wedding band. I had never noticed it before. "Kom." This time I did not disobey him.

His master bathroom was beautiful, all dark marble and black fittings, best of all her pictures were not here. I was glad, it seemed sacrilegious to do anything in her presence. He stood before me, and as the water filled the large Jacuzzi he undressed me ever so slowly. He was much better at foreplay than his brother was, I hated to admit this. He was calmer and more experienced, he took everything slow, delighting in lingering pleasures.

He removed my top, I had nothing on under it, his eyes alighting on my inner arms and the ugly scars there. I realized he had not sighted them before, he ran his fingers over them, they tingled. "What is this?" He looked at me earnestly, his grey eyes searching my face for the answer.

I looked to the floor trying to lose myself in the patterns in the marble, I would not speak of that dark time to anyone. I could not. He continued to undress me like I was a small child, tenderly, slowly. He never pressed me for an answer like Master would have. He then undressed as well and guided me to the bath. The water was warm, relaxing, and unlike bathing with Master this bath was large, luxurious and deep. The water came up to my chin. He sat opposite me drinking his wine that sat perched on the rim of the tub.

He was heavier set than Master, slightly less defined, but still very handsome. His hair was slightly thinner and longer, a shade darker than Master's was, he had many intricate Oriental tattoos on his shoulders and arms. The designs all flowing onto the other, they were on further study very beautiful. I had never looked at this man so closely before, I had always been afraid.

He shifted his position in the tub closer to me, I heard the grandfather clock in the great room chime midnight, a clear resonant sound. He pulled me onto his lap, the water sloshed and spilled from the sides of the tub, he was every bit as strong as Master was. I did not fight him and let this quiet, gentle, man do as he wished. I had never felt so calm. He looked long at the tattoo on my belly. "He should not have done that to you. There is a time and a place." Was all he said. Yet he had locked me up in Master's absence. I did not understand.

He kissed me lightly on the neck and the face. I closed my eyes and unlike that first time many months distant, I did not pull away. To my surprise I found I was reciprocating his kisses in kind, and they progressed from light fleeting touches to deep kissing on the mouth. He loved me in a way Master never had, he truly saw me, the real Myra. Not an object, not a slave, not a platform to fueling his own ego. Just me the girl I really was. I cried tears of astonishment and joy.

He lifted me from the bath, and tenderly dried my tears. "Do not cry Myra." He said in his awkward English, smiling at me, he had the same, winsome, smile as his younger brother. He dried me off, and wrapped me in his oversized, black bathrobe. I had not felt this way since I was a little girl. I watched him carefully, sitting on the bath mat like a lost refugee, he was a magnificent man. He was Master, yet older, wiser, and kind.

He guided me into the adjoining Master bedroom. I stopped to look at her picture that graced the bedside cabinet. "May I ask her name?" I could not help my curiosity, reminders of her were everywhere.

"Ona." He replied, as he turned back the covers on the bed. He seemed not at all upset to utter her name, or speak of her. His four poster bed was very high, I had some difficulty climbing in and maintaining some sense of dignity. He just watched me and smiled, I sensed he was glad not to be alone. He turned out the lamp and lay beside me. "Tired?"

"Yes," I said, and I was.

He pulled me into his embrace, finally letting me settle my head beneath his solid arm. I could hear the beating of his heart, it was most comforting. My eyes closed and I realized in one of my last thoughts before sleep took me I could understand his words much better than I had before.

My dreams were fitful, convoluted, and dark. They we so bad I woke, I was ashamed to say I was begging, begging them to stop. I still revisit the river shack often, it plays over and over and I can never find an ending I can stomach. It is an unfinished terror that inhabits my nights. I woke him, he was not annoyed with me like Master would be. He comforted me and I returned to sleep.

When I did wake it was late, at first I sat up and could not fathom where I was. I had become so used to Master's four walls it had almost erased memories of anything else. I slid out of the tall bed, I was unsure what was expected of me, out of habit I pulled on my blue blanket and quietly stole through the house. The soft clean carpets felt good under my feet, unlike the threadbare floor coverings of Master's home. The walls were lined with art, beautiful photographs, and sculpture everywhere, even a grand piano shining black, with real ivory keys. Out of sheer curiosity my fingers plucked the notes, I cannot play but I had always wished I had learned. Other girls at school had, but not I.

"You are awake finally." He had been in his office.

I jumped at his voice, snatching my fingers from the piano, feeling like a criminal. "I'm sorry Sir." I stammered.

He smiled leaning in the office doorway. "It's quite all right Myra. You had a bad night?"

"I'm sorry, Sir." I said again looking at my toes. He walked towards me soundlessly on the carpet. I felt his fingers under my chin.

"Look at me Myra?" I did, it was hard to, his gaze was very bit as intense as Master's. "Come lets get something to eat. I am sure you are hungry, and I want to talk to you."

I followed him to the kitchen, he made me sit on the bar stool. It felt so very wrong to not be serving him. It took all my will to stay where he had asked, I did wonder if it was indeed some trick that he might punish me for later. He made toast, eggs and bacon, and tea for me while he had coffee. He even remembered how I liked it, white with no sugar. I was at once sorry I had bit him. His kitchen was like everything else he owned, shining and orderly, and I found myself wondering how he kept his home so clean?

He tore me from my practical musings with his unexpected words as he pushed a plate of food towards me. "Now I want to know truthfully Myra, if my brother asks for you to return, and he will shortly. Do you want to go?" He sounded ever so serious, all I felt was trepidation. I was most fearful to answer him. It had been a long time since anyone had asked me what I wanted, or thought. Silence was my friend, he was Master's brother after all. "I'm serious Myra, what do you want to do?" I could not frame an answer and did not try. I sat and ate instead. He did not press me but continued nonetheless. "I know you are scared Myra." He touched my wrist, I was not expecting it. I thought he was going to grab me and I jumped. He was faster, he held my arm on the cold granite countertop. "Tell me what happened Myra?" His fingers gently caressing the livid scars. "Did he do this?" His grey eyes on me. I tried to pull my arm away from his scrutiny, but he did not relent holding me fast. I nodded no, but did not utter a word. "I see." He seemed disappointed. "I can't make you talk Myra, but if you want to talk I will listen." I nodded, he released my arm. I hid the shameful scars under my blanket. I was sure he could make me talk anytime. I knew Master could.

It was a strange day, he never ordered me to do a single thing. I felt lost and bewildered, with no sense of purpose. He spent most of it in his office, the phone rang frequently and he sat a long time at the computer. I do not think he had word from Master at all, and if he did he did not tell me.

That evening he called me to him. I had still not even thought to dress. I was so unsure what this man wanted from me. I did not dare do anything, nor touch anything. I was hungry, but thirst gnawed at me more than my need for food. He stood bare chested, arms crossed, in the centre of his sumptuous living room, so like Master I shivered with fear as I slowly approached him. He was different then he had been last night toward me.

"After my conversation with you earlier today Myra I can see I will have to use a different approach. I understand what it is my brother has done. I just did not understand how profoundly it had affected you. I know him well, probably a lot better than you do. Sit." He pointed to the floor before him, I knelt at his feet. He was tall and mighty above me. I examined his toes in great detail, he could have been Master if I did not look up. So I concentrated on that, it was easier on my mind if I could view them as one and the same man.

He sighed, he seemed bothered. I hoped he was not displeased in me. His bare feet fidgeted on the carpet. "Lose the blanket." He said, his voice not so soft any more. I was certain now he was displeased, I did as he requested immediately. I did not look up. "You are not my slave Myra, you are only entrusted to me. I wish it were different, but it is not. However right now you are under my roof and my protection." I quailed at his utterance, he sounded so like Master I was afraid to hear where this was leading. I was sure from experience more of the same. "Show me your arms." It was not an optional request. "We are going to talk about that." I stretched my arms out before me on the white carpet palms facing up, my shame bared to him. I was most glad to look at the floor and his feet, I do not think I could have looked him in the eye.

"Why at only eighteen would a young girl do this to herself? Answer me Myra." I did not answer, silence was my friend. I repeated it over and over to the exclusion of all else. My mantra, my salvation. His words and his presence I could, and would blot out.

Blinding pain ripped me from my safe place, he had hit me just as Master did with his belt. I had been so engrossed in hiding in my special place I had not even noticed he had moved. "Tell me Myra." His voice did not harbor any malice. He had made a mistake, one Master never did. He did not know me intimately, Master always tied me when he hit me, and he had not.

I shot up from the floor and ran, I do not think he was expecting it. He should have after the last time. His house was sprawling and two story, much larger than Masters and very unfamiliar. Surprisingly I evaded him for many long moments. He knew his home better than I and cornered me in an upstairs bathroom, he closed the door.

"Tell me Myra." My worst nightmare, he was not going to relent. He stood tall, his broad back pressed to the door, there was no escape. He crossed his arms and looked at me with great seriousness, his stubborn manner frightened me. He was impossible to thwart, even with all I had learned. He was in many ways cleverer than his brother. "If it takes all night. I will wait. I can make you tell me Myra, but I would rather you chose to." I sunk slowly to the floor in the shower stall. The cobalt tiles were as cold as his grey stare. I could not tell him, I must not. The tears began innocuously at first, if only he would leave me alone. I put my hands over my face trying to stifle my emotion but the tears would not stop.

He was by me on the floor crouched on the tiles, large, benign, and warm. All I could do was cry loudly and unashamedly, he held me and said nothing. He was like my grandmothers blanket, comforting and warm. I cried into his furry chest. He picked me up and carried me downstairs and I remembered how thirsty I was. I did not have to ask, as he deposited me on his large leather lounge and brought me some water. He shook his shaggy blonde head and sighed, but thankfully did not press me further.

Much later after I had recomposed myself he brought food, it appeared unlike Master, this man could cook at least simple meals. I cannot remember a man ever serving me in all my life. I found I had little stomach for food, I had thought I was hungry, but was now in too much inner turmoil to eat more thaw a few bites. He watched me while he ate everything on his plate, he even ignored the phone in the office. He put the china down, wiping his short beard on the napkin, everything he did was with a steady deliberation, it was calming to me.

"Do you like music Myra." I nodded an affirmative. He turned on the CD player. "So do I." He took the plate from my hands, putting the leavings of our meal on the sink. I made to get up, I am sure he would want me to clean up. I had been very lax in his home. "No Myra, it can wait." He studied me for some time and sat at the other end of the lounge, the leather creaked as he sat down. "You are most beautiful Myra in your innocence, and the way you are so unashamed. I can see why he covets you."

I realized I had made no effort to cover myself. I was unhinged, yes I was. I know it would be all to easy to just forget. To venture out in public unclothed, like a mad woman in some classic story. Master had done this to me, by slow degrees I had accepted it as the norm. "So køn Myra." His words were tender, almost reverential. I wished Ona's photos had not been present. I let his warm hands wander where they chose.

The phone rang by the bedside table, it woke me with a start. He reached blindly for the receiver in the dark. "Svend Eriksen." He answered, still groggy from deep sleep. Listening to the disembodied voice on the phone I think I knew instinctively who the caller was. "You did what! Shit, you can be so fuckin stupid." More from the earnest male voice on the other end, I could not catch the words. "Look brother the drive is three hours." He sounded exasperated. "I will not be there until tomorrow, you need to cool off." He set the phone down on the voice with a resounding click. "Sleep Myra, it's going to be okay." He patted me on the thigh and turned over, he was snoring in minutes. I cannot say the same. I lay awake listening on the hour to the chime of the grandfather clock, until the pale dawn announced the new day.

This morning I made him breakfast and cleaned away last night's mess, he came into the kitchen dressed and ready for the road. His expression went from resigned and most serious, to a smile on seeing me. I so wanted him to tell me what had happened, but I knew not to ask. He sat at the bar and ate, downing the strong coffee. He leaned forward over the granite top. "I know you are a good girl Myra. So, I would like you to give me your word. While I am gone today I want you to stay here, inside. Do you think you can do that?" He was asking me nicely, I had not forgotten the time he had imprisoned me in the basement.

"Yes, Sir."

"I want more than that Myra. I want you to promise." He also would seek to bind me in the chains of my honor, just as Master had. However I did not relish the alternative of being locked up. He had done it once, I assume he would have no trouble doing it again.

"I promise I will not go outside Sir."

"Very good Myra, I am going to hold you to that." He smiled, a warm smile that did reach his eyes. "You do realize you can wear clothes." He chuckled. I had not thought I was allowed to.

"Well, I'm off to Copenhagen, I should be home by dinner time. There is food in the fridge, use what you like, he pointed to the television, and even at the computer in his study. "I would prefer right now if you did not call anyone. If you want to talk to your mother perhaps we could do it tonight. I can trust you can't I?" He looked at me sternly. I nodded, I could not believe he was going to allow me all these liberties, what did he want from me. I hoped it was at a price I could pay. He picked up his car keys and patted me on the head. "Be good Myra, for me." Some things never changed.

"I do not want to do this Myra but I must." He sighed, it was a troubled sound. "Frej has asked for your return." It was late Tuesday evening and my spirits plummeted with his words. I was just beginning to enjoy my new surroundings, and even more disturbingly, him as well. It was one thing to fulfill a duty to him as a slave, but I felt more, so much more. Master would not be at all pleased with the new thoughts in his slaves head. I did not know how I would cleanse myself, but I sensed it would be a painful cleansing indeed. "I have had a very good talk with Frej. He has promised me things will improve greatly. He told me to tell you he thinks he has his house sold." I did not know what this would portend but I hoped it would indeed be an improvement in our life together. "I have some sites to overlook in Kobenhavn, so I will take you back tomorrow." I must not cry, was all I could think.

There he was framed in the doorway, I swallowed and got out of the car, slowly I walked up the cracked cement path, the weeds had broken through it in many places, the grass was long and unruly, there were no flowers. For the first time I registered Master's life was absent of beauty, so unlike his brother's home. I prayed it would soon change.

The two brothers stood facing one another, they did not speak. I could feel the tension pass between them like electricity. Master looked at me his black eye making him look ever rougher and more evil than he usually appeared, the white of it was bloody. He sported some large cuts on his face, one above his left eye, the other high over his cheekbone. They had been stitched and I was sure they would scar his clean, handsome, visage.

I had heard the story related patiently to me by his brother during the long return drive. Master in his drunken anger had assaulted someone in a bar, then had been arrested and had to be bailed. It was most fortunate he worked for his father's company, he would have risked his good employment had he have of been working for anyone else.

Master retrieved my bag from the pavement. "Go inside." He ordered, his tone hard, and I immediately regressed to who I had been just days before. I stood in the lounge room turning in slow circles, the house was most disorderly. Every room, every surface was in disarray, I breathed deeply and held my tears in check, determined today he would not make me cry. I could hear the two brothers talking in low monotones. I could not make out what they said.

His boot heels resounding on the floorboards behind me. "Just four days with him and you forget all I taught you!" The excruciating slap followed in quick succession to his angry statement, as he slammed the door and threw my bag down. I tore off my clothes in panic and knelt before him on the floor, he had not changed in the least. He seemed more fierce and uncompromising than I had ever remembered. I trembled at his feet, I was saying sorry. He kicked me in the ribs, I fell to my side winded. I looked up at him, this was how he liked things, me helpless and begging for his mercy. I was not ashamed, beg I did. I did not need his hurt. He stood above me obviously aroused by my pleas, they were real and heartfelt. Oh to be anywhere but here at this moment.

I broke under his hardness I cried to him, I entreated him, I wanted his love, not his black hate. He pulled me from the floor, he wanted love too but not at all in the fashion I did. There was no clear space on the floor so he threw me on the unmade bed, he tore off his blue jeans and used me with such roughness and iciness I did not know him. He was so forceful I did not even have the breath to cry.

I lay beside him in the wreckage of his home, listening to his ragged breathing subside. Before I knew it he was asleep, and I wondered if during my absence he had not rested at all. I already knew the answer. I shivered, even though his large body next to me was warm. I did not have to be told he could not function properly without me by his side, it was my duty, my sacrifice, to keep him sated, that other innocents may not have to pay his price.

I spent the remainder of the day restoring order to the mess that was his home. He slept soundly, nothing woke him, not even the vacuum nor the cool breeze that blew over him from the opened bedroom window. I stood beside him as he slept in the iron bed, he was oblivious to me or my intentions. I was going to cook some dinner. I had been cutting meat and I realized the futility of it, as he would not be stirring this evening.

The sharp meat knife was still in my hand as I stood over him looking at his cut face, and bruised countenance. He looked like a savage animal. My thoughts strayed back to how I first beheld him on that far distant July day, golden, strong and pure. The shining knight who would free me from all my woes. Today as I looked at him he was none of these, all I could see was perverse and twisted hate. I don't know what madness gripped me then, and I will never know. I thought of all the women who had ever been, like me, pushed, controlled, and made to fear a man, to perform his every dark desire. I wanted to cut him; Myra the girl who could not utter the simple word no, yet I felt this sudden surge of blinding, hateful desire.

I did not need reasons, but I listed them just the same. They read like a death warrant. The baby, Cleo, the tattoo, the river shack, my diminishment of sexual pleasure, the isolation, the terror, and Gabrielle. I had never met her, but I felt her pain acutely and before I knew it the point of the knife was on his skin. He did not stir. I cast it to the floor and ran away, horrified of that which I had even considered. Evil begets evil, and I had just borne witness to it.

He was standing before me the next morning, in his hand the incriminating knife. I had fallen asleep on the lounge, the sleep of the troubled it was. Broken and riven by terrible dreams. I woke with a start, he was calm and rested. He did look a lot better, I wished I could have said the same for myself. "What is this?" He waved the blade at me, its sharp threat too close to my face.

"I don't know how it got there?" I said reflexively and woodenly, with the suddenness of the convicted. Even though I knew lying to him was not a viable or clever option.

"Hum........." I could see him looking at me with narrowed eyes, he was not sure if he believed me or not. "Breakfast, bitch. I'm late."

BLIND OBEDIENCE

Things were different now between us, guilty thoughts assailed me at every turn. When he used me I closed my eyes and thought of his brother. The two men almost interchangeable in the darkness, though only physically. His home repelled me, I had now seen better than the mold filled grout on the bathroom walls, and the cockroaches in the kitchen sink. The torn linoleum, threadbare carpets, and peeling walls.

Something had happened between Master and his brother also. Something monumental, every night without fail he would call and demand to hear me tell him I was in good spirits. Master resented this I could tell, but in his desire to have me returned to him he had agreed to his brother's terms, and he adhered to them with a gruff reluctance.

I could tell he did not trust me as he had before, he had also changed the rules, and life had become very hard. Last Friday evening he had returned home from work, he limped slightly now when he was tired I noticed. I greeted him as I always did, and thought nothing of looking up at him as he sifted through the mail. I always did. He rose from the chair slowly, deliberately. I knew he was angered but I did not know what I had done. Nothing different or out of the ordinary.

"Remember Tubby?" He asked. I nodded, the thought of her disturbed me even now. He went to the spare bedroom I could hear him looking for something. I did so wish he would not tear the place apart every time he wanted some simple item. He returned with a stout length of bamboo cane clasped in both hands. My heart sank, I did not think I could take many more of his rigorous new strictures. "It's time you mastered blind obedience." It sounded ominous, if only he would stop I cried internally in my despair. Outwardly I prepared for his wrath. "A good slave will kneel in place for her punishment, she will accept it without being tied. You Myra, have always been a willful slave. It is time you changed your ways. A good slave will only speak when told to speak, she never speaks out of turn as you do........ And a very good slave like Tubby." He poked me with the cane. "Will not raise her eyes to look at anyone."

He had said that night long ago he would never reduce me to this. Face to face we had sat and he had told me so, now he had turned on his word. Words of steel could be broken, and so could I.

He sat in his chair waiting for the phone. Tapping the cane on the leather to mark the slow passing of time. The timing of his brother's call was very predictable most evenings, perhaps that was his failing. Master was too wily to hit me before he had called, and I had assured him I was being treated well. I knew if my mouth had betrayed me his brother would have been too far away to have come to my rescue until it was much too late. I played the game just like we all did. I wanted to cry when I heard his voice on the phone, but he was in Arhas miles away.

Master closed his phone with a flourish and put it back in his pocket, he rose from his chair. He put the music on loud enough to cover any noise I might make. "To the basement." He instructed, and I knew tonight's lesson would be a savage one. He had never insisted we go down there before. I knelt on the damp floor, the small stones and debris dug into my knees. I knew in a few moments I would not feel it. There was no point begging, I knew he would not listen.

"DON'T LOOK AT ME!" The cane came down across my lower back sharply, I gasped. The pain lingered for long moments. Everything in me screaming to run. I did not. I tried to master my fear, eyes to the floor. "From tomorrow you will be a new slave Myra, an obedient one. I will have no more lip from you, understood." The cane arced and fell again, one agonizing stroke of hot fire to join the ache of the one previous. "Not only that." He pushed the tip of the bamboo under my chin and made me look at him. He was not the man I knew, he was a beast, an unbridled monster, why had I not seen it so clearly before? "You are NEVER to look at me again unless I direct you to. Never, understand. Eyes to the FLOOR!" This time the cane was applied in earnest, three more blows, he held nothing back. I was writhing in pain.

"Now that we understand each other I want you slave to tell me about the knife. You lied to me the other morning didn't you. I don't like lies." I had not expected him to raise this matter again, I had shelved it, it was something I was deeply ashamed of, a flight of madness I would not revisit. "What did you expect to do with it Myra?" I wondered then if he had indeed been watching me feigning sleep. Cold fear gripped my soul, silence would not help me. "You really think you could hurt me with a knife. Do you, little you?" He laughed, it was a dangerous velvet laugh.

"I'll tell you what Myra. I'll make you a deal. If you can hurt me with the knife I will set you free." I felt sick as I studied the dirt on the stone floor. The same knife fell in front of me and skidded in the dirt. "Go on Myra I know you hate me, pick it up." I did not move. He hit me again, five more strokes, I could not take too much more of this and I found I could not hide inside myself, not this time. I angered him by my inaction and passive stance. I thought he was making to leave but he turned and laid into me savagely with the cane. This time he did not relent nor did he hold back. I lost count of the strokes my world only gauged by searing pain.

His anger spent he left me laying on the damp, cool floor in the dirt. I found I had no tears. It could never be the same between he and I. I would play his game, I would be as he wanted, always pleasing. I would feign his blind obedience as he put it, biding my time until I could get out. One day his brother would rescue me, I had to hold on to that.

Master had not sold his home at all, but had leased it to Mick. It was easy and expedient and meant he did not have to erase all traces of his nefarious activities such the crude cell in the basement, and for Mick it was a selling point. It allowed Master to get on with his new plans for us with immediacy. To that end he had been studying endless real estate brochures of some very pricy homes in Arhus. Could he afford them? I was not sure. They were even grander than his brother's lovely home. He did not ask me for my opinion on any of them, all pretense of love for me was gone. I had well and truly descended into naught more than flesh for his abuse.

I could have run away I guess, perhaps I should have. Part of me was too afraid to try, and I had no idea what would happen if I did go to the police. It was not just Master who was implicated in this, and would be viewed in a bad light. Master's brother would certainly come under scrutiny as well, and I could not do that to him, so I suffered on. I had no wish to hurt him, especially. I was glad Master was fixated on living in Arhus, I would be close to the one man who could extract me from my life of untold misery. I found he was in my mind often I thought of his tenderness, his patience, his gentle love. Even in my darkest moments he gave my strength to push on just one more day.

TWISTING THE CHAIN

It was a fine Friday evening and she stood there on the front porch, in her trademark short dress and stilettos. Today she wore passionate red, it matched her fiery hair. You could see plainly by her body language she did not wish to be here. Master's working class address was beneath her high standards, and pedigree. Tall and proud as always she reminded me of a show horse. Always groomed, always beautiful, every hair in perfect place.

He stood there with her. I watched them from the window, it was open and I could hear them plainly. He made to kiss her and she stopped him with a deft movement of her hand, almost burning him with her cigarette. "When are you moving?" Was all she said, blue blood coursed through her veins. She looked out at the street impatient to be gone, grinding the leavings of her cigarette into the concrete on the front porch. Nothing ruffled her cold exterior. They were two of a kind. However even I could see she played the game at a higher level than he.

"Soon, when you decide which house we should buy." Did I detect humility in his voice? She laughed, it was a cruel rippling sound and she turned to smile at him, her lipstick was ruby red, her makeup unblemished.

"There is only one I liked." She shot back. "You know which one." He said nothing. Most unlike him. "Impress me Frej and I will reconsider your proposal," she added flippantly. "I'm going to be in Paris for the next week, I have a shoot there. You can tell me all about it when I return." She deigned to kiss him then. He paused, and I could sense his hesitation. His words always spoken with such authority and sureness tumbled out of his mouth. He sounded like a schoolboy.

"Tell me Birgitte....... If I buy it, tell me you will?" He was begging, I could hardly believe my ears.

I could feel his pain acutely, he had done this to me many times in just the same fashion. I could tell Master wanted so much more than her brief parting gesture, a mere brush of her lips on his, he was used to getting what he wanted. However Birgitte did not give him any more than the most fleeting hint of pleasure, and she was in her convertible and gone. I wondered what happened to his theory that all women were merely created, to be the slaves of men?

He stood long moments on the front porch watching her drive away down the quiet street. Her perfume lingered, mingled with her cigarette smoke. The cooling breeze blew his long, golden hair. Even though it was high summer it never felt warm here, unlike the long lazy summers of Alabama. I missed them, I felt homesick. He sighed and his proud shoulders slumped, plainly he was addicted to what he could not have. I wondered where this would lead.

Master had spent a troubled night. I had lain in bed drifting in and out of fitful sleep, and he had paced the house until the small hours of dawn. Things were weighing heavy on his mind. I was up early, he had finally crawled in beside me, he was invitingly warm but I did not linger in the bed. I went to the kitchen my feet cold on the floor, my blanket about my person. I still bore marks from the cane, and he had added new ones in nights past, for any deviation from his edicts no matter how minor. I was making toast and tea, he would not be up for some time yet. I could be myself for a little while longer. He always lingered in bed on the weekends often sleeping until noon, and I found I relished these stolen moments of peace.

I gazed at the table, there were many documents laying there and a glossy magazine beneath them. I sat at it, the old chrome chair squealing as I pulled it across the worn linoleum. I drank my tea slowly, it was very hot, but still one of the simple joys of my day. My behind was aching dully as I sifted through the papers on the table top. They were of course all worded in Danish, but I knew enough to see the one I was looking at was a contract, and it had his name signed on it in many places. There were many brochures as well, all of homes in Arhus, pricey, elegant. I guess he had chosen then, as I looked at his signature scrawled on the clean white paperwork, and I would go where he took me sight unseen.

I pulled the glossy magazine out from under the plethora of real estate brochures, it was not something I usually saw him with. I flicked through it's pages, again it was in Danish, but the images were sublime and colorful. I paused and put down my cup, there she was Birgitte, larger than life in a lingerie commercial, sultry, sexy, beckoning all the world to have her. She really was a model.

I closed the book. I was shocked and yet I was not, Master might have looked like a rock star, but she was the real deal. Could he even begin to keep up with the pretense of wooing a woman like that?

My slavery is now one of open abuse and rigid control, he makes every effort to enforce on me I am here for three reasons, to cook, clean, and open my legs for him. That is the sum of my being. He is in love, but not with me, all he sees is Birgitte. Sometimes I dare peek at him when he does not notice, he is troubled and dark, restless and agitated. His anger simmering just below the surface he is always ready to strike me.

It appears he has retreated from his friends for the most part, and his brother as well. I rue this, and wish it were otherwise, it has been almost three weeks since I last saw him. All I can cling to is the sound of his voice in his nightly calls on the phone.

August the final flurry of summer, which to me has not been summer at all, opens. Master is readying to move, he and Mick spent the entire weekend removing the contents of the basement. I was thankful Mick did not bring Tubby, but I did wonder where she was at this moment, imprisoned somewhere, given to another jailer? She as I, could never be free.

The clean up was a huge task, the two men labored many hours to bring the heavy items upstairs and out into the yard. The majority of it Master threw way in the large dumpsters that lined the alley way behind his home. If I had expected to see any skeletons secreted down there of his past I was disappointed, it was all very ordinary. The heavy work hurt Master's still healing leg, bringing on his limp. In the evenings it would trouble him, he would stretch it out on the ottoman and I would dutifully massage it, while he drank and talked with Mick. If Mick held any resentment over the fact Master would not share me he did not show it. I did not look at him, but I could feel his dark eyes on me constantly, they made me shiver.

"She seems better behaved." Mick announced as he stubbed yet another spent cigarette out in the ash tray and reached mechanically to light the next one. He was worse than my father. I wished he would not comment on me, he was like a vulture, I could sense he was always hovering hoping for Master's juicy leavings.

"I've been into her." Master said coldly. He moved, I knew without looking he was pointing to the cane that had now taken up permanent residence a top the mantle, over the long disused coal burning stove. Both men laughed, it gave me cold comfort.

I spend my last days here, all his possessions are packed. There are very few he will take with him. We live these last days here with just the bare necessities at our disposal. Fortunately he has pressing bookwork so his computer is still available to me. I am grateful for small mercies. He has all but cleansed himself of his old life. Even his dented Fiat with mismatched panels has made way for a new car, a shining cherry red Corvette ZR1. There were many fine European cars he could have bought, Porsche, Mercedes, Ferrari to name only a few, but I guess he was influenced by his stay in America more than I had thought. Somehow the decadence of my country suited him, he was in many ways more American than I.

ALL THINGS MUST END

    I did something so foolish today I am sick with my fear. I accidentally clicked on the profile of someone I should not have, a simple slip of a mouse to be my undoing. It was none other then the friend of my Master's in Alabama, my protector, who had looked after me in my Master's absence. All I can hope for is he does not log on, which knowing him is highly doubtful. He will know who I am, and who I refer to instantly. I cannot believe this has happened. I usually do not linger to look at profiles. I guess it was fate, some sick twisted form of it sent to betray my lies to Him.

    Oh, Noctiserus!
You hold all my hopes and lies in your hand...........

    I sit here for what is very likely the final time I shall be able to be at liberty to do so. I feel like Anne Boleyn, tragic second wife of King Henry the eighth as she calmly crossed the tower lawns on that fateful day of May nineteen 1536 towards the swordsman; he who would be her executioner. Master will know soon of my transgression and like many women before me throughout history, both spoken of or forgotten I will pay his price, whatever he will demand of me.

    I would like to thank you all, each of the wonderful, selfless, people who listened, cared, and gave me such comfort in my confusion and self doubt. Some of you saw in me a victim, some an uncertain child, some a sister or daughter, and some of you merely a blind object of desire that they wished to own themselves.

However understand this, as I once told someone here with great passion. All my life I was told by many I was spineless, worthless, and I could not continue my resolve, nor be strong. I do not plead guilty, for I am none of those. Yet I am his slave in body, mind, and spirit. I understand the meaning, I know the associated costs. I will not break under the yoke he would place on my back. I will go to him, admit my betrayal of his and my intimacies. I will be irrefutably his. That being said I wish you all the most wonderful things in the world, and I bid you all as it is said in the Danish language, "Farvel" Goodbye.

I will kneel tonight naked and trembling in his magnificence, I will stand worthy of his slave steel. I hope your thoughts will be with me. I shall my friends, draw strength from you all................

Thank you for listening Myra.